Dancing
with
Dennis Hopper's Ghost

A Fernando Lopez Santa Fe Mystery

DANCING
WITH
DENNIS HOPPER'S GHOST

A FERNANDO LOPEZ SANTA FE MYSTERY

JAMES C. WILSON

SUNSTONE
PRESS
SANTA FE

Sunstone books may be purchased for educational, business, or sales promotional use.
For information please write: Special Markets Department, Sunstone Press,
P.O. Box 2321, Santa Fe, New Mexico 87504-2321.
Printed on acid-free paper
∞
eBook: 978-1-61139-767-3

Library of Congress Cataloging-in-Publication Data

Names: Wilson, James C., 1948- author | Wilson, James C. 1948- Fernando Lopez Santa Fe mystery
Title: Dancing with Dennis Hopper's ghost : a Fernando Lopez Santa Fe mystery / James C. Wilson.
Description: Santa Fe : Sunstone Press, [2025] | Series: A Fernando Lopez Santa Fe mystery | Includes reader's guide. | Summary: "When a dying Jack Lacy, a professional assassin, returns to Santa Fe wanting to be buried near his friend Dennis Hopper's grave in Jesus Nazareno Cemetery outside Taos, former Santa Fe Police detective Fernando Lopez helps arrange a crossover ceremony so Lacy can join Dennis Hopper's ghost, but after the ceremony Lacy's body disappears and Lopez has to find Lacy among the living or the ghosts in order to give him a proper burial at Jesus Nazareno Cemetery"-- Provided by publisher.
Identifiers: LCCN 2025050457 | ISBN 9781632937759 paperback | ISBN 9781632937766 hardcover | ISBN 9781611397857 epub
Subjects: LCSH: Hopper, Dennis, 1936-2010--Fiction | Taos (N.M.)--Fiction
Classification: LCC PS3623.I58485 D36 2025 | DDC 813.6--dc23/eng/20251215
LC record available at https://lccn.loc.gov/2025050457

WWW.SUNSTONEPRESS.COM
SUNSTONE PRESS / POST OFFICE BOX 2321 / SANTA FE, NM 87504-2321 /USA
(505) 988-4418

PREFACE

Under the mystery plot, the ghosts and the crossover ceremonies, *Dancing with Dennis Hopper's Ghost* is a very personal story of human mortality and the passing of a generation. Dennis Hopper's Taos years coincided with my Santa Fe years. Indeed, I spent a couple of afternoons at the Mabel Dodge Luhan House when he owned it, though I don't remember seeing him there. Typical of his/my generation, Dennis was as wild as a tornado and often as destructive, but he found something in Taos that meant a great deal to him. Sure, he occasionally ran afoul of the Taoseños because of his behavior, but many years later that something brought him back to Taos to be buried in the humble Jesus Nazareno Cemetery. Likewise, that something brought me back to New Mexico after thirty years of teaching at the University of Cincinnati. Santa Fe in the 1970s was where I became who I am. It's where I discovered what I valued and what I wanted to do with my life. Because of this I owe Santa Fe a great debt and it's why I consider myself a Santa Fe writer. All the characters in my Fernando Lopez Santa Fe Mysteries are based on people I knew there in the 1970s. I consider my mysteries love letters to Santa Fe and Northern New Mexico.

"You get used to the dark, you realize the ghosts are all friendly."
—Jack Kerouac, *Desolation Angels*

LAST CALL

John Hammond banged his beer glass on the bar at Santa Fe's historic La Fonda Hotel demanding a refill, while his companion Lou Vigil slouched over the bar, sound asleep.

"You boys have had enough. We're closing in a few minutes anyway," the young punk behind the bar said, pointing to the wall clock on the side wall that read one minute until Midnight.

"Hell no, I'm still thirsty, gimme one more for the road," John replied, an old hippie and community activist who'd been active in the recent *entrada* riots and who'd risen to prominence as far back as the La Raza and Vietnam protests, half a century ago. With his long gray beard and ponytail, complemented by his ragged jeans and white T-shirt that read "Fight the Power," he looked like a down-on-his-luck derelict or an escapee from the psychiatric hospital in Las Vegas, New Mexico.

The baby-faced bartender shook his head. "We're closed. Now get the hell out of here."

John poked Vigil in the ribs, rousing the old timer.

Vigil raised his head. "Are we leaving?"

Pissed, John got up off his stool and stumbled, pitching to his right into Vigil. He caught himself on the bar momentarily and stood up straight. "You wanna fight?" he said to the bartender.

"Fight who?" Lou mumbled, looking up at John.

"I'm talking to him," John said, pointing to the bartender.

"Look," the bartender said, raising his voice now, "you get the hell out of here or I'm calling security."

"All right, all right...gimme a damn minute," John said. He helped Vigil get to his feet. "Come on, Lou...the bastards don't want us here."

"Fuck 'em," Vigil mumbled, hanging on to John as the two of them shuffled into the lobby. The bimbo at the front counter gave them the Evil Eye as they staggered around the corner and out the front door of La Fonda. The streets and sidewalks were deserted, not a soul in sight. Not even a damned tourist!

Outside they rested against the side of the hotel for a moment, steadying themselves for the trip home. Then John moved away, leaving Vigil leaning against the building by himself. Just then a taxi drove up in front of La Fonda. John noticed the taxi had an Albuquerque license plate. Must be an airport shuttle from the Sunport in Albuquerque. He also noticed his friend Vigil staggering down the sidewalk, with his left hand still on the side of the building for support. Vigil disappeared around the corner of Old Santa Fe Trail. Old Lou couldn't hold his liquor the way he used to. Getting old was a bitch.

Just then the rear right door of the taxi opened and out stepped a tall, lean man dressed all in black, including his fedora and a three-quarter length wool coat. Wealthy, very wealthy, John figured. Must have cost a small fortune to take a taxi at this hour of the night from the Sunport to Santa Fe, sixty miles away. The man in black reached into the taxi and pulled out his black carry-on suitcase and then paid the taxi driver. When he stepped away, the taxi sped off up San Francisco Street and then turned right onto Cathedral Place.

John approached the stranger, planning to take advantage of this unexpected opportunity. "*Hola!*" he said, waving.

The man in black stared at John, not moving. His fedora, pulled down over his forehead, masked his face in shadow.

"Jonathan Hammond at your service," John continued, not about to give up. "May I take your bag, give you a nighttime tour of downtown Santa Fe or, for a small fee, point out some of the many sites that make our unique city famous."

The stranger continued to stare at him, not speaking.

When John reached out and touched the man in black's shoulder in what was meant to be a friendly gesture, the stranger recoiled and snarled, "Get your hands off me, you scum!"

John grabbed the man's arm and opened his mouth to respond, but before he could the stranger pushed him away. While John staggered, trying to restore his balance, the stranger opened his waist coat and pulled out a long-barrel pistol with what looked like a silencer on the end of the barrel. He pointed it at John, who tried unsuccessfully to duck.

The pistol made a zipping sound when the stranger pulled the trigger, the last sound John would ever hear.

The force of the bullet hitting his forehead knocked John backwards. He fell hard onto the concrete sidewalk into blackness.

1

Former Santa Fe Police Detective Fernando Lopez sat on his patio watching the yellow leaves on the cottonwood trees in his back yard glitter in the wind. A cold wind today, now that October had arrived with a dusting of snow on the Sangre de Cristo Mountains east of the city. Not even his North Face jacket kept him warm outside, which meant his morning brooding sessions on the patio were coming to an end. Too bad, because he did his best thinking sitting on the patio, overlooking the cottonwood trees and Estelle's rose garden.

Begrudgingly, Fernando grabbed his coffee and cell phone and walked back into the kitchen, where he tossed his jacket on one of the chairs at the kitchen table. He refilled his coffee cup and went back to his study to finish his early morning brooding. He sat at his desk and pushed back his laptop, not wanting to spill coffee on it. No doubt about it, he'd become a brooder. After thirty years of police work and another five as a private investigator, who wouldn't brood? Too many bad memories and things he regretted. He called himself a 'fixer' these days, semi-retired but still taking an occasional case helping friends and acquaintances clean up their messes. There was never any shortage of people who needed help cleaning up their messes, especially among his artistic friends on Canyon Road, where his former office as a private investigator had been located. He actually enjoyed his work as a fixer because he had more leeway as a fixer, not constrained so much by the law. More flexibility, so to speak. Being a fixer also allowed him to work at home. No need for an office. Better to keep the business on the down-low.

Fernando had the house to himself this morning. Estelle, his wife of nearly forty years, had already left for work at the Saint Francis Immigrant Outreach Program, a church nonprofit that provided food and clothing and other services for the ever-growing number of immigrants stopping in Santa Fe, a Sanctuary City. They stopped but didn't stay long because it was much too expensive to live in Santa Fe these days. Hell, local Santa Feans could no longer afford to live in Santa Fe.

Estelle wanted him to retire completely, which was ironic because unlike him she worked every day Monday through Friday at the Outreach Program. Sometimes she even worked on the weekends. The fact of the matter was that both of them needed to keep busy. To keep from going to the Dark Place.

His last two cases—Peyote Circle and Stealing the Hopi Snake Dance—had exhausted him. He planned to relax for a while and catch up with a number of small house repairs he'd been postponing. Estelle had given him a list, which he had conveniently mislaid (tossed in the trash, that is). Now that he had the time, maybe he could work up some interest. Maybe.

He finished his third cup of coffee and was about to get up to brew number four when his cell phone buzzed on the desk. He saw the familiar name on the screen and clicked accept. "What's up, Manny?"

"Morning, Fernando," Manny Alvarez replied. Manny had replaced Fernando as lead detective at the Santa Fe Police Department. He still consulted with Fernando when a case involved people they both knew. "I don't know if you've heard yet this morning, but your old friend John Hammond was gunned down last night about Midnight in front of La Fonda."

"Old John Hammond? Who would want to shoot him?"

Manny laughed. "Probably everyone involved in everything he protested against as a community activist for the last thirty or forty years. He was like a pit bull—he never let up."

Fernando laughed too. He knew very well that Hammond could be a real pain in the ass. He'd gotten his fill of the old hell-raiser during the *entrada* riots, which Hammond had helped instigate. Fernando didn't know for sure, but he suspected Hammond was also involved in pulling down the obelisk in the Plaza because its inscription ran afoul of a bunch of newcomers who preferred political correctness to history. He hadn't seen Hammond since, thankfully.

"Turns out John had been drinking all evening with Lou Vigil in the La Fonda Bar," Manny continued. "According to Brad Lewis, the bartender that night, both of them were drop dead drunk. He shut off both of them and kicked them out just before Midnight."

"What did Vigil say?" Fernando asked. "Was he with Hammond when the shooting occurred?"

Manny sighed. "Not exactly. He heard the shooting, but he was already walking away down San Francisco Street. He described the shooter as a huge demon, a monster dressed all in black with no face."

"No face? What the hell is that supposed to mean?" Fernando asked.

"Hah! Good question," Manny said. "I should have prefaced my report by saying that Vigil is not your most reliable witness, even when sober. When we talked to Vigil this morning at his home, he was experiencing bad DTs—I mean he was shaking like an old washing machine. His wife and extended family had gathered at the home and were about to take him to a rehab facility on Saint Michael's Drive to detox. He looked like he was pretty far gone."

"I've never met Vigil, but I know John was a heavy drinker, always had been," Fernando said. "Especially back when he was raising hell about the *entrada* a few years ago."

"So that's all we know at the moment," Manny said. "We don't know if it was a random or a targeted shooting, and we don't know if the shooter lives on the street or is staying at La Fonda—nothing."

Fernando leaned back in his chair and shook his head. "Jesus, Hammond must be eighty years old by now. What a way to go."

"Anyway, I wanted to let you know, since you and John go back a long way," Manny said.

"Thanks. Keep me updated," Fernando said and clicked off.

2

Fernando knew John Hammond only too well. The man had been a thorn in his side all during his time as lead detective for the Santa Fe Police. Hammond had been instrumental in the movement to abolish the *entrada*, the parade during the annual Santa Fe Fiesta that celebrated the reoccupation of Santa Fe by Don Diego de Vargas in 1692, twelve years after the Pueblo Revolt drove the Spanish out of Santa Fe. He'd also been involved, if not one of the leaders of the mob that protested and finally pulled down the obelisk monument to Union soldiers on the Santa Fe Plaza. The Hispanic community in Santa Fe was especially pissed at the 'cancel culture' that Hammond represented, the desire to tear down tradition and history.

For sure, Hammond had lots of enemies, but why would someone want to shoot him now, when he was a harmless old drunk? He hadn't been active in Santa Fe politics for a couple of years now. Didn't make sense, not to Fernando anyway. Which meant the shooting must have been a random encounter with the wrong person, maybe a street person, as Manny speculated. Or maybe a teenager out for kicks or drugs. Or someone who had a personal grudge. Not that it really mattered to Fernando. This wasn't his case—he had no skin in the game.

So with that thought freeing him from worrying about the shooting, Fernando decided to read the *Independent*. Anything to avoid beginning his home repairs. He found the newspaper on the kitchen counter where Estelle had discarded it before leaving for work. He took the newspaper into the living room and hunkered down on the sofa to read it. No mention of the Hammond shooting, which had occurred well past the *Independent's* deadline.

When he finished reading the newspaper Fernando tossed it in the trash where it belonged. Then he made a beeline for the kitchen, intending to make an early lunch. On his way to the kitchen he heard his cell phone ping in his study, where he'd left it on his desk. He was surprised to find the text was from his best friend and former colleague at the Santa Fe Police, Sergeant Antonio Blake, who had recently retired and moved to Alamosa, Colorado, where he was helping his son run a ranch he'd recently inherited from his maternal grandparents.

Fernando hadn't seen or even heard from Antonio since his Peyote Circle case earlier this year, when Antonio was struggling with a reoccurrence of his Post Traumatic Stress Disorder. For relief Antonio was taking peyote and attending a peyote circle run by a quack therapist and drug pusher for patients suffering from anxiety and/or PTSD. According to this and other therapists, peyote induced visions that helped distance and often free the patients from their anxieties and traumatic memories. Unfortunately, a patient was murdered during one of the peyote meetings and Antonio was suspected, wrongfully, of committing the murder. Fernando took the case and managed to prove Antonio's innocence after an exhausting journey filled with mayhem and murder. As soon as his name was cleared, Antonio decided he'd had enough of Santa Fe. He abandoned his cabin in the Pecos Wilderness and joined his son on his son's ranch near Alamosa, Colorado, PTSD and all.

Fernando opened the text and read: "Back for one day. Need to see you. Room 316 La Fonda. Urgent."

Urgent? That didn't sound like Antonio, who was perfectly capable of taking care of any situation by himself. At six feet eight inches and two hundred eighty pounds, Antonio had been known as the enforcer down at the Washington Avenue Station. He intimidated everyone, including his colleagues when he worked at the Santa Fe Police Department.

Worried about his old friend, Fernando decided to head down to La Fonda right away. He glanced at himself in the hall mirror to make sure he was presentable, which was contrary to his longstanding aversion to looking in the mirror. He firmly believed that he aged every time he looked in the mirror. Sure enough, when he glanced in the mirror today he noticed more wrinkles in his face and more salt than pepper in his short-cropped hair. His flannel shirt and jeans were reasonably clean, though. That was good enough.

He locked up the house and climbed into his Cherokee. Even the Cherokee was cold today; the ignition turned over a few times before the motor caught. He drove down to the Paseo and around to Alameda

Street, where he usually parked when he came downtown. Since the summer tourist season was long gone, he found several available parking spaces along the Santa Fe River. He plugged his meter and walked up Old Santa Fe Trail to San Francisco Street. The main entrance to La Fonda was just around the corner.

When he walked through the heavy wooden doors he looked for the hotel manager at the front desk. Fred Mondragon had banned Fernando from La Fonda for most of the year, after several of his lunch meetings with clients in La Plazuela had turned ugly, with shouting and chairs flying. None of it was Fernando's fault, but he'd had a hard time convincing Fred of that. Then, last month, he'd managed to sneak in for a peaceful lunch during his Hopi Snake Dance case and Fred seemed to give him a reprieve after he discovered Fernando's presence, or rather his transgression. Seemed was the operative word. He didn't want to press his luck.

As it turned out Fred wasn't at the front desk when Fernando entered La Fonda, so he didn't have to worry about Fred. He took the stairs to the third floor and walked down the long hallway to Room 316. When he knocked he heard someone walk to the door and look through the peep hole. Same old Antonio, always a bit suspicious, if not paranoid. Then the door swung wide open and Antonio reached out and grabbed Fernando, pulling him into the room.

"Well, it's nice to see you too," Fernando stammered as Antonio gave him a bear hug.

Antonio looked great. He'd lost a bit of weight around his waist, but his arms were even more muscled and his shoulders bigger. He could have been a linebacker in the National Football League if he'd chosen.

"Thanks for coming," Antonio said, closing the door after first looking up and down the hallway.

"No problem. Damn, it's good to see you, Antonio," Fernando said. "How's the PTSD? Are you still taking peyote for it?"

Antonio patted the leather pouch on his belt. "It's better, I can at least live with it now, thanks to the peyote."

"How's your ranch working out?" Fernando continued. "And how's your son? Lotta questions I want to ask you."

Antonio raised his hand. "All in good time. At the moment we just have to get the hell out of here."

Puzzled, Fernando said, "Out of here? Didn't you just get here?"

"Yeah—I drove down from Alamosa last night when I got the call," Antonio replied. "Left about Midnight and drove all night. Got in about six-thirty, before the day shift arrived."

"I guess I don't understand," Fernando said. "You didn't come to visit—for a vacation?"

Antonio shook his head.

"Why then?"

At that moment the bathroom door opened and out stepped a tall, emaciated man wearing all black, shirt and pants. He looked like a skeleton draped in black, with a hollowed-out skull and deep black circles under his eyes.

Fernando did a double take. Something about the man looked familiar. The clothing?

"Fernando, do you remember Jack Lacy?" Antonio asked.

Fernando's spirits sank. His mouth fell open.

Before him stood Jack Lacy, known to local law enforcement as the Santa Fe Assassin.

3

This Jack Lacy bore no resemblance to the Jack Lacy Fernando remembered from just one year ago. Then he recalled that Lacy had told them he suffered from Glioblastoma or brain cancer as a result of Burn Pit Exposure in the First Iraq War. Lacy and Antonio were old war buddies, having served in the same Marine unit, Lacy as a top-ranked sniper. Trained to kill, Lacy had continued his work as a hit man for hire after leaving the military, a paid assassin making enormous sums of money killing corrupt businessmen and politicians for other corrupt businessmen and politicians in the Mideast and Eastern Europe. Lacy always said he only continued doing what he was good at, what he was trained to do in Iraq.

The sight of Lacy now triggered an unpleasant flashback. Last year Lacy had arrived in Santa Fe on an assignment to assassinate a high-ranking government official from Washington who was to appear at a public ceremony. When the ceremony had to be cancelled, Lacy refused to return the six-figure advance he received from his employer, who then hired another hit man by the name of Archivada from the Sinaloa Cartel to either get the advance back or kill Lacy. Thus began a shooting war between Lacy and the Sinaloa Cartel in Santa Fe. Both Antonio and Fernando were drawn into the war because of Antonio's long friendship with Lacy. The war came to a bloody conclusion at an A-frame on Upper Canyon Road, after the Sinaloa Cartel kidnapped Antonio and offered to return him only in exchange for Lacy's advance.

Fernando remembered the shootout. He'd arrived at the A-frame carrying a bag of newspapers instead of the money Archivada had demanded while Lacy had positioned himself with his sniper's rifle on a trail in the National Forest looking down on the A-frame. He saw the scene unfold in his mind as if were only yesterday:

Fernando scanned the area around the A-frame, looking for potential gunmen hiding on the grounds or in the upper windows of the A-frame. He saw nothing that raised suspicion. So he honked the horn of the Cherokee and held it for several long seconds. Then he climbed out of the vehicle carrying his duffle bag. He stopped a few feet in front of the Cherokee and dropped the duffle bag in the dirt. Then he waited, feeling like a sitting duck. Like a goddamn fool.

Moments later Fernando saw shadows moving inside the front window. Eventually the front door moved slightly and then opened wide. Archivada himself appeared in the door. With his low-cut shirt and the gold chain hanging from his neck, and especially with his black hair slicked back with gel, Archivada looked like an old fashion gangster in mafia movies. Archivada nodded when he saw Fernando standing near the duffle bag. He held the door of the A-frame wide open and said, "Good. Now bring the bag here."

Fernando held his ground. "No. Bring Antonio out first."

Archivada frowned. He looked behind him and then turned back to Fernando. "Bring the bag here and you will have what you want. Your friend is alive and well, just inside the door."

Fernando panicked. He looked around, not knowing what to do. Lacy expected him to bring Archivada and the others outside where they would be vulnerable. Cursing, he blamed himself for not having a backup plan. He knew better. At the moment all he could think to do was call Archivada's bluff.

Desperate, he grabbed the bag and turned around, walking slowly back toward the Cherokee.

"Wait!" Archivada called. "Your friend is here."

Fernando turned around, still holding the duffle bag.

Antonio appeared in the doorway, standing beside Archivada.

"Come get him," Archivada said.

Fernando shook his head and continued walking away, ignoring Archivada.

"Okay, wait!" Archivada shouted. He stepped carefully out of the A-frame, looked around, and walked slowly toward Fernando holding what looked like the key to Antonio's handcuffs in his hand. Antonio followed a few steps behind, pushed and shoved along by Archivada's two gorillas. The younger of the two kept poking a pistol in Antonio's side. Antonio snarled at his tormentor, swinging his elbows to push the man and his pistol away from him. For a moment Fernando thought Antonio was about to turn on his tormentor, but the big man controlled himself. Antonio wasn't used to accepting physical abuse.

Finally Archivada stopped about thirty feet away from Fernando. He smiled, full of confidence, as if he'd just won the jackpot.

Fernando stared at Archivada, not moving. Expressionless.

"Give me the duffle," Archivada said.

Suddenly a loud explosion erupted from the hill above: Crack!

Instantly the top of Archivada's head exploded, showering Antonio and the two gorillas with bright red blood. Archivada fell backward, landing in the dust.

Then all hell broke loose. The two gorillas ducked, searching the hills above for the shooter. The one with the pistol fired off a couple of wild rounds that ricocheted off the rocky cliff.

Crack! Crack! came the retort from above.

Dropping his pistol, the younger of the two gunmen grabbed his chest and crumpled to the ground.

Instantly Antonio pushed aside the other gorilla and then grabbed him from behind, pulling his handcuffs tight around the man's neck. Half a foot taller and at least eighty pounds heavier, Antonio lifted the smaller man off his feet, choking him. The man's legs dangled in the air, kicking wildly. Not finished, Antonio jerked the man's head back so violently that Fernando heard the neck snap like a twig. Then Antonio dropped the dying man, who lay twitching in the dust for a few brief seconds before falling still. He didn't move again.

Free of his tormentor, Antonio scrambled over to Archivada and pried open his hands to get the key to the handcuffs. Fumbling with the key, he shouted to Fernando, "Watch out, there's two other guys in the house."

Just then gunfire erupted from the A-frame: Pop! Pop! Pop! Pop!

Bullets ripped up the ground in front of Fernando and Antonio, who crouched behind Archivada and the other two bodies. While Antonio unlocked his handcuffs and threw them aside, Fernando sighted the two shooters just inside the door. They took turns stepping out in the doorway and firing wildly, then retreating inside to reload their pistols.

Lying flat, Fernando snuggled up against the gorilla with the broken neck. He placed his arm across the dead man's chest and steadied his Smith & Wesson, waiting for one of the shooters to jump out into the open door. Suddenly the dead man's body began to twitch slightly, as if trying to wake up. Another jerk and then the dead man's muscles relaxed. The energy, like air, seemed to drain out of the body once and for all. Leaving just a cadaver, not a person.

Fernando squeezed off a round: Pop!

His bullet shredded the right side of the door frame.

"Fuck this," Antonio said, standing upright and taking aim at the door. When the gorilla on the left side of the door appeared, he and Antonio opened fire at the same time. The gorilla fell backwards. Antonio pitched forward, dropping the gun.

"Are you hit?" Fernando asked.

Antonio held his right hand against his stomach. "Aww, shit," he said and then shook his right hand as if trying to shake out the pain.

Fernando saw the hand was bloodied. He tried to get a close look at the wound.

"It's nothing," Antonio said. "Bullet just nicked my fingers."

"Here," Fernando said, handing Antonio a bandana he always carried in his rear pocket.

Antonio wrapped his hand in the bandana. "It's payback time. I got one more to deal with," he said, motioning toward the A-frame.

Fernando grabbed Antonio by the shoulders. "No, you stay here. Let me do this. You can't use a gun with your hand like that."

Before Antonio could protest, Fernando headed for the A-frame. He crouched low moving off toward the left side of the building. When he reached the front, he stood flat against the logs and shimmied over to the door. He listened for any movement inside but heard nothing. Then he peeked in the door and saw the dead Sinaloa gunman lying on the floor. Beyond the crumpled body the entryway and front room were both empty. No sign of the other shooter.

Moving as quietly as possible, Fernando slipped through the door and fell to one knee, scouring the front room and hallway for any sign of the second shooter, who seemed to have disappeared. Not a trace. So Fernando moved carefully into the long hallway, taking one small step at a time. Now he saw the kitchen in the rear of the building.

Suddenly something crashed in the kitchen. Sounded like pots and pans all hitting the floor at the same time. Fernando froze against the wall.

Then the shooter bolted out of the rear kitchen door. As Fernando watched, the runner stumbled on the porch outside and fell in the dirt. Then he scrambled up and took off running around the back of the A-frame.

"Stop!" Fernando shouted, running outside.

The shooter turned and fired a shot at Fernando: Pop!

The bullet thudded into the logs over Fernando's head. He ducked back inside the kitchen door. Moments later he heard a car engine start. He ran outside and around the A-frame just in time to see the shooter drive off in the Toyota Sequoia. Fernando crouched and tried to steady his aim, but the Sequoia was moving too fast for him to get a good shot. Too late.

Then he saw Lacy. The man in black had walked halfway down the hill overlooking the A-frame. The Grim Reaper himself. Down on one knee, Lacy had a bead on the Sequoia, following it in the scope of his sniper rifle. As the big vehicle entered the clearing near the end of the driveway, a shot rang out in the canyon and echoed loudly: Crack!

Instantly the Sequoia began to swerve to the right. Slowing to a crawl, it rolled off the driveway into a stand of yellow chamisa bushes and came to a stop, engine sputtering.

Lacy stood up, put the SAKO on his shoulder, and continued on down the trail as though nothing out of the ordinary had happened. Just another day at the office. Another kill.

Fernando picked up the handcuffs that Antonio had discarded and then waited for Lacy at the bottom of the trail. "Hell of a shot."

Lacy nodded. "Easy with the SAKO. It's dead accurate up to eleven hundred meters."

"Well, that depends on who's shooting it," Fernando said.

Lacy smiled. "Yes it does."

They walked together across the parking lot to the Sequoia, which had finally stalled when the vehicle came to rest in the bushes. Antonio was already standing there, holding his bleeding hand against his chest. He motioned to the Sequoia. Not a pretty sight. The bullet had shattered the rear window and blown through the driver's neck, almost severing his head from his body. The impact had left him slumped over on the right side of the steering wheel. Blood dripped from the front windshield and dashboard and pooled on the floor mats.

Then Lacy mumbled a feeble greeting to Fernando, bringing him back to the here and now. The tall, emaciated man dressed all in black slowly shuffled over to a Queen Anne chair in the corner of the room. Grimacing, he eased himself down in the stuffed chair and started gasping for breath. The short walk from the bathroom to the chair had exhausted him.

"We need to get Jack out of here before the manager sees him," Antonio said to Fernando. "You remember our incident in La Plazuela?"

"You mean when Lacy had a melt-down and jumped up from the table screaming that he saw ghosts?" Fernando replied. "Yeah, I remember. It got me banned from La Fonda."

Fernando didn't have much sympathy for Lacy until he noticed all the bottles of medication on a table between the two Queen beds, including opioids. The man was clearly in a bad way.

"Jack flew in to Albuquerque last night and took a taxi to Santa Fe," Antonio said. "He checked in just after Midnight. The night shift didn't notice him—who he was, I mean."

Suddenly Lacy started coughing. He doubled over and then sat back in his chair wheezing. Spittle oozed from his lips.

"Okay, but why's he here?" Fernando asked.

Antonio nodded. "He's on his way to Taos. He wants to find a curandera—or curandero—who can cure him or, if not, help him cross over. Then he wants to be buried in Jesus Nazareno Cemetery as close as possible to Dennis Hopper's grave. He was a friend of Hopper's, as you might remember."

Fernando did remember the connection. Lacy said Hopper had given him some important advice when he came back from Iraq alienated from his own country. He remembered Lacy saying he was lost and confused and couldn't understand the hostility toward him and the other veterans. Lacy said he and Hopper had spent a day drinking, during which Lacy had told him, "Fuck it! You don't owe your country anything. They turned you into an assassin. That's your country now." That turned out to be the beginning of Lacy's career as a professional assassin.

"Remember, we took Lacy to Jesus Nazareno Cemetery to see Hopper's grave before taking him to the airport?" Antonio asked.

"I remember very well...and I remember what Lacy said about Dennis Hopper's advice," Fernando replied. "But I don't know about Jesus Nazareno, which is strictly a local cemetery. I think you have to either live in Taos or have some connection to the place in order to be buried there."

"Well...he's ready to pay whatever price they want, up to fifty or even a hundred thousand dollars," Antonio said.

"Or...more," Lacy croaked from the chair where he was sitting.

Fernando shrugged. "So what's your plan? How can I help?"

Antonio laughed. "I don't have one. You're the one who always came up with the plans. How do we get him out of here?"

"Is there a back elevator?"

"Yeah, but it's only for staff. You need a key," Antonio said.

"Well, hell, then just take the front elevator and walk out, Fred Mondragon won't stop you," Fernando said. "Believe me, he'll escort you out himself, if he sees you. We'll all go down together and the two of us will try to stay between Lacy and the front desk. They might not even notice us."

Antonio smiled. "See, I knew you would come up with a plan."

"Not much of a plan," Fernando replied. "Where are you parked?"

"I'm around the corner on Shelby Street."

"Then I'll wait with Lacy outside the front door while you go get the car. You can pick him up there and be on your way."

Antonio nodded. "What about you?"

"What do you mean?" Fernando asked.

"Aren't you coming? I could really use your help in Taos. You know the area a lot better than I do."

Fernando's spirits sank even lower. He should have known. They wanted him to help out in Taos, the last thing he wanted to do. Partly because Estelle would be furious if he tried to explain why he had to go to Taos yet again. He'd spent way too much time in Taos on one case after another since he'd closed his office as a private investigator and announced he was retiring. He figured being a fixer would be something he could do while retired, but fixing other people's messes had turned out to be more involved than he originally thought.

Still, he couldn't say no to Antonio. The big man had saved his ass more times than he could count. He had a debt to pay.

So Fernando decided to suck it up and do what he always did: send Estelle a text from Taos, after the fact.

"Okay, when do you want to leave?" Fernando asked, glancing at Lacy. "He doesn't look like he's in much shape to travel."

"Right away—as soon as we get packed," Antonio said. "I made a reservation at the Mabel Dodge Luhan House. I reserved Mabel's bedroom and the Gate House Cottage in case Jack can't climb the stairs to Mabel's bedroom. I think the Luhan House is a good place to stay if you want to be anonymous in Taos. Maybe even better than the Sagebrush Inn."

"Whatever you say," Fernando said, not eager to return to the ghost-ridden Luhan House. Too many bad memories of the Mud Palace, as Dennis Hopper called it when he lived there in the 1970s. Too many ghosts.

He took a seat on one of the queen size beds and watched Antonio pack Lacy's carry-on suitcase, careful to get all Lacy's medications together in a small nylon case that went inside the suitcase. Lacy just sat in his chair and watched Antonio work, looking as though he were about to fall asleep.

When Antonio finished packing, Lacy struggled out of his chair and walked to the closet, where he put on his long black waist coat. Then he shuffled over to the table between the two beds and opened the top drawer, taking a long-barrel pistol out of the drawer and slipping it in the pocket of his coat. Looked like a 357 magnum Colt Python, a badass gun.

"Whoa...we don't need any guns here," Fernando said. Guns in Lacy's hands meant dead people wherever he went.

Lacy turned and gave Fernando a hostile, don't-mess-with-me look. "Nobody takes my guns away."

Antonio raised his hands to quiet the disagreement. "Let's go," he said, helping Lacy to the door.

Fernando followed them down the hall to the elevator, where they waited. When the door opened an elderly couple stepped out, eyeing them suspiciously when they noticed Antonio holding Lacy upright.

Inside the elevator Antonio hit the button for the first floor. None of them spoke. When the door opened, they saw a handful of people gravitating to La Plazuela, La Fonda's first floor restaurant. Following their plan, Antonio and Fernando tried to hide Lacy behind them as they slowly made their way to the front door. They would have made it if Lacy hadn't tripped and pitched forward. Fortunately Antonio caught him, but the commotion caught the attention of the front desk where Fred Mondragon and his staff stared at them.

Someone yelled, and instantly Fred ran out from behind the front desk into the lobby area. He opened his arms wide and mouthed, "What the fuck?" You didn't have to be a lip reader to catch the drift of what Fred was saying.

Fernando turned and waved at Fred. "We're leaving...don't worry!"

Fred just stood there shaking his head and watching until the three of them managed to exit the hotel.

"Okay, wait right here with Fernando, I'll drop off the key card and go get my Wrangler. I'll be right back to pick you up," Antonio said to Lacy, turning the man in black over to Fernando and walking off fast.

Fernando tried to hold on to Lacy, but Lacy snorted and shook him off. Instead of Fernando, Lacy leaned against the side of the building. Which was fine and dandy by Fernando.

Minutes later Antonio's Jeep Wrangler roared to a stop in front of La Fonda. Antonio jumped out and helped Lacy into the passenger's seat. He buckled Lacy's seatbelt as he would a child's

Fernando deposited Lacy's suitcase in the back of the Wrangler and stood back out of the way.

"Meet us at the Mabel Dodge Luhan House," Antonio said as he climbed into the driver's seat. We'll be in the Gate House Cottage."

Fernando bit his tongue. He wanted to say no thanks. What he really wanted was to tell them to go to hell. Instead, he waved.

As he watched them drive away, Fernando had mixed feelings. He had no illusions. He knew exactly what he was doing: aiding and abetting the person who shot and killed John Hammond last night.

Helping a murderer escape.

4

Back home Fernando rummaged through his bedroom closet and found the duffle bag he used for short trips. He packed his shaving kit and a change of clothes, just in case he had to stay overnight. Not what he wanted to do, but it was better to be prepared. Writing his note to Estelle, he took his time and chose his words carefully: "Antonio is back in Taos. He asked me to come up to help him with something, don't know what. Be back tonight or tomorrow. Love, Fernando." Not exactly the truth, but close enough, he decided.

Then he gassed up the Cherokee on Cerrillos Road and headed for Taos. He took Highway 84/264 to junky Española and then turned north on Highway 68, the so-called Low Road to Taos. The highway followed alongside the Rio Grande as it snaked its way through green triangular hills spotted with piñon and juniper trees. One of his favorite drives. The High Road to Taos through the mountains was probably more scenic, but he loved to see the river and its many rapids glinting in the sun, the lifeblood of New Mexico

The seventy-five minute drive gave him plenty of time to think about Jack Lacy's aborted first visit to Santa Fe, where he had almost single-handedly killed Archivada and ended the Sinaloa Cartel's presence in Santa Fe. During that time Lacy had some sort of crisis and began seeing ghosts everywhere, including the disastrous lunch in La Plazuela that got all of them banned from La Fonda. Antonio and Fernando finally persuaded Lacy to leave Santa Fe, but not before Lacy insisted on making a quick trip to Ranchos de Taos to visit Dennis Hopper's grave in Jesus Nazareno Cemetery. Turned out Lacy and Hopper were friends and that one night when they'd been drinking all day, Hopper had given Lacy some advice that had changed his life. Or so Lacy claimed.

Now Lacy apparently wanted to join Hopper in Jesus Nazareno Cemetery. For eternity.

All of it was a bit much for Fernando, who had no love for Lacy. When healthy, Lacy had been a cold-blooded killer, the most dangerous man Fernando had ever encountered.

Approaching the Rio Grande Gorge Visitor Center he heard a text ping on his cell phone, which he managed to read while driving. The text, from Antonio, read: "Checked in. Gate House Cottage. Luhan House."

Soon he entered Ranchos de Taos and passed by the massive San Francisco de Asis church. The beautiful church had been photographed and painted by dozens, if not hundreds of artists.

Entering Taos, the highway ahead seemed to run straight to the deep blue Taos Mountains on the horizon. He plunged down the big hill, passing the Sagebrush Inn on his left. The road became more congested as he approached the historic Taos Plaza. Bypassing the Plaza, he turned right on Kit Carson Road and then left on Morada Lane. The sprawling Mabel Dodge Luhan House sat back from Morada Lane on the right side of the road. The name of the place was somewhat deceptive because the property included multiple buildings. The big adobe house, built on a slight rise, overlooked several smaller buildings below, some of them used for guest quarters and others in a perpetual state of disrepair: the Pink House, Tony's House, and the Gate House Cottage, among them.

Fernando turned into the large parking area, empty except for a couple of cars parked near the stairs up to the big house and Antonio's Wrangler parked over by the adobe gate on the southern side of the property. He pulled up beside the Wrangler and climbed out of his Cherokee, leaving behind his duffle bag in the hopes that he wouldn't have to spend the night. Wouldn't it be nice?

Not surprisingly, the Gate House Cottage was located next to the southern entrance to the property. A small adobe building, the Cottage came with its own enclosed patio complete with wrought iron furniture. He spotted Antonio and Lacy sitting at the patio table under an umbrella as he walked into the Cottage. Access to the patio turned out to be through the master bedroom, a cramped little room with heavy wooden furniture that looked handmade. Antonio waved as Fernando walked onto the patio, glad to have company.

"Not bad," Fernando said, looking around the patio and back at the bedroom. "What'd this cost you?"

"About three fifty for the Gate House Cottage and another two fifty for Mabel's bedroom," Antonio said.

Fernando frowned. Seemed like a waste of money to him. "Why Mabel's bedroom? Isn't there enough room here?"

"Yeah, but Jack wants to use Mabel's bedroom to meditate and try to communicate with Dennis Hopper. Hopper owned the Luhan House in the seventies, you know. He slept in Mabel's bedroom on occasion."

Fernando started to reply but then stopped, not wanting to offend Antonio or Lacy. Why bother? Better to hold his tongue. He knew a lot more about Hopper's stay at the Luhan House than Antonio or Lacy. He'd even been here a few times in those heady counterculture days when he was single. He and several of his buddies had come up to the Luhan House on occasion to listen to the music and enjoy the seemingly endless supply of free weed. The place was always crowded, but they never encountered Dennis Hopper himself.

"I know you're skeptical, but Mabel's bedroom has a long history of ghosts," Antonio said. "Ghosts of Mabel and Tony and lots of others have been recorded throughout the house, but especially in Mabel's bedroom. People walking and talking in the room when no one was there, doors opening and closing, chairs moving, stuff like that."

Sitting slumped in his chair, Lacy nodded his head in agreement as Antonio described the recordings made by a paranormal organization in Taos.

Again, Fernando said nothing.

"Jack wants to go over about two o'clock, after his nap," Antonio said. "There's some stairs...so he'll need help."

Lacy mumbled something dismissive.

"Anyway, we stopped at Albertsons on the way in and bought some supplies—coffee, beer, milk, bread, sandwich meat and cheese, even some frozen dishes to microwave. We have a full kitchen here, so help yourself."

Moments later Lacy managed to stand up by himself and walk into the adjacent bedroom. He sat on the edge of the big bed and then gingerly eased himself down on the mattress. Not long after he lay down Lacy started to snore softly. His breathing was labored.

While Lacy slept, Fernando and Antonio talked.

"Thanks for helping," Antonio said. "Jack doesn't have anyone else. Nobody. He just wanted someone to be there with him at the end.

Someone sympathetic. I didn't know if I could do it alone, so I called you. I hated to bother you, but you're the only person around who knows Jack."

'Knows Jack' struck Fernando as a gross exaggeration. He knew next to nothing about Lacy.

Still, Fernando raised his hand in protest. "No problem. It's okay. I'm happy to help out."

"Must be a bitch to not have anyone to call—to die alone," Antonio said. "That's one of the reasons I moved to Alamosa to be with my son. To have someone to be with me at the end."

Fernando nodded. Even though he sometimes didn't act like it, and he certainly didn't like to talk about it, he was eternally grateful for Estelle and their two daughters, Flavia and Adela. What would he do without them?

"I thought maybe we could eat some peyote and then go with Jack to Mabel's bedroom and see what happens...what visions we have," Antonio continued. "You've done peyote and know what to expect. I find the visions free me...and help me better understand whatever problems I'm having."

"I guess...." Fernando replied, not as enthusiastic as Antonio. True, he had done peyote on a number of occasions with one of his cousins who happened to be a member of the Native American Church, whose members used peyote regularly—and lawfully. He just wasn't as convinced as Antonio of peyote's restorative powers. Nor did he like the feeling of losing control. Some people found that freeing; Fernando found it paralyzing.

"We might even talk to Dennis Hopper. Here, take one," Antonio said, holding out his leather bag with a stash of dried brown peyote buttons inside. Looked like twenty or so buttons.

Fernando took one button. Antonio took two.

5

Later, after a short nap, Lacy awoke and sat up in bed. "I'm ready," he said. He managed to get out of bed by himself and shuffle into the living room where Fernando, and Antonio were talking.

"For Mabel's bedroom?" Antonio asked, even though he already knew the answer.

"Right...I need to check in with Dennis," Lacy said.

Fernando was already nauseous from eating the peyote. He felt light headed and a little dizzy. Fortunately he didn't feel paralyzed because he hadn't yet experienced any visions.

The three of them went outside and walked across the open parking area to the Luhan House. Antonio helped Lacy up the stairs and into the courtyard of the big house, a sprawling century-old adobe structure that contained some two-dozen rooms on the first and second levels. A partial third level rose above the rest of the house like a tower, complete with rows of windows, some hand-painted, overlooking the grounds. None other than celebrated English novelist D. H. Lawrence, the author of *Lady Chatterley's Lover,* was rumored to have painted a couple of the windows. Vegas, chimneys, and iron weather vanes cluttered the patchwork roof creating a bizarre, slightly ominous Gothic look.

Fernando had stayed at the Luhan House during his Taos Gothic case a few years back. In that case a Santa Fe historian had been murdered, ostensibly by ghosts, while researching Willa Cather's stay at the Luhan House in the 1920s. He had the same reaction every time he saw the discombobulated Luhan House. It looked as if the house had no design but was instead assembled one level and one wing at a time by someone who happened to be stark raving mad.

The sidewalk took them up to a long flagstone porch under a veranda. They stepped inside a corner doorway and entered the central part of the house—sitting room, dining room, and kitchen, all appointed with furnishings that looked decades old. As soon as they were inside a prideful Lacy swatted away Antonio's arm and walked, unsteadily, by himself. Needing, but not wanting, to be helped.

Fernando followed, keeping his distance. Bad memories of all the dead bodies from his Taos Gothic case flooded his mind, haunting him. Lots of them from this and other cases after thirty plus years in law enforcement. That was the thing people didn't understand. You could be haunted by bad memories every bit as much as actual ghosts, probably more, since bad memories are more common and would seem to be more numerous than ghosts. Sometimes it seemed that everywhere he went stirred up bad memories.

To the right of the sitting room a familiar woman sat at a desk in what passed for the office, a tiny room no bigger than a walk-in closet with a desk, book shelves, and file cabinets crammed into the small space.

"Hello, can I help you?" she asked Antonio and Lacy, a dapper older woman with short gray hair wearing a tailored black suit that fit her perfectly. She smiled when she noticed Fernando coming up behind Antonio and Lacy. "Why, hello Fernando...it's been ages," she said.

"Hi Francis," Fernando said, remembering her name now from his last visit. Francis Rose.

Antonio explained that Lacy would like to use Mabel's bedroom for meditation, as they had discussed earlier.

Francis nodded. "Of course, the stairway to Mabel's bedroom is over there," she said, pointing to the hallway. Then she glanced at Lacy and asked, "Do you need any help getting up there?"

"No!" Lacy blurted out. He turned and walked away by himself, apparently offended by the question Francis had asked. Antonio hurried to catch him as they reached the ancient stairway, while Fernando stayed at the front desk for a moment to apologize for Lacy's bad manners.

"No problem. I know he's not well," Francis said. "Your friend Antonio said he suffered from Glioblastoma. That's nasty stuff."

"It is," Fernando agreed. "He has only weeks, maybe just days to live."

Francis clucked her tongue.

Fernando thanked her and hurried to catch the others before the peyote kicked in. Once that happened, climbing a rickety stairway might be tricky. His vision was already starting to blur at the edges.

The wooden floorboards creaked and groaned as the three of them climbed the steps to Mabel's bedroom. Antonio held Lacy's left arm. Fernando followed behind in case Lacy fell, as if he were in any condition to catch someone falling down the stairway on top of him.

Like this they stepped onto the upper landing. Lacy shook free of Antonio and walked quickly into Mabel's bedroom, a light airy room with Mabel's enormous bed set between two large windows flooding the room with sunshine. The cheerful sunshine seemed out of place in the dark gothic surroundings. The bed frame itself was hand-carved with four enormous posts the size of fire hydrants on each of the four corners of the bed. Small tables, both appointed with lamps, sat on either side of the bed in case there wasn't enough light from the windows.

Not hesitating, Lacy took a seat in a red Queen Anne chair off to the side of the bed and sat there for a long moment taking a series of deep breaths and looking around the room. "Leave me alone, I need to talk to Dennis now," Lacy said. "I'll call you when I'm done."

Antonio, confused, looked around the room. "Is Dennis here?"

"Of course he's here," Lacy snapped, irritated by the question.

Fernando nudged Antonio's arm. They quietly left the room and made their way back down the steps to the ground floor. Antonio led the way into the living room, crowded with furniture and multiple fireplaces. They sat in leather chairs beside the nearest of the adobe fireplaces, this one built next to a carved wooden post that supported the ceiling. The adobe fireplace, painted white, extended out into the room. A large pile of freshly cut firewood sat off to the side of the fireplace waiting for colder weather. Already the old, drafty house was none too warm. He could tell that winter would be a bear here.

"How long will he meditate?" Fernando asked, shaking his head, his patience running low.

Antonio shrugged. "He said a couple of hours."

Fernando was already tired of Lacy and his demands but didn't see any way to extricate himself from the situation without offending Antonio. Antonio had become Lacy's manservant. Or so it seemed.

"Did you see anyone else in that room?" Antonio asked.

Fernando laughed. "You mean a ghost? No."

"Do you believe in ghosts?" Antonio asked.

Fernando said the same thing he always said when asked this question, which was often because New Mexico happened to be cursed—or blessed, depending on how you looked at it—with an abundance of so-called haunted places. How could it not be haunted, with three separate cultures often at odds with each other for going on five hundred years?

"I don't know," Fernando said. "I neither believe nor disbelieve in ghosts, but I know I saw something—a ghost, a specter, whatever you want to call it—at Chaco Canyon and Painted Skull Ranch and elsewhere."

Antonio nodded. "I remember Painted Skull Ranch."

Fernando continued. "But to answer your question, it makes no difference whether they exist or not. The imagined world is just as real as what we call the real world," he said, tapping on the side table next to him. "If you believe in ghosts, the thought of being around one changes you psychologically and physically—you get anxious and paranoid, your pulse quickens, your blood pressure rises, and so on. Understand what I'm trying to say? It makes no difference. What matters is what you believe."

"I get it," Antonio replied.

"Lacy believes in ghosts, so for him they exist—or might as well exist, if you want to look at it that way."

"Well, if you're looking for ghosts, you won't find a better place than this," Antonio said. "Creeps me out." With that the big man stood up and walked out of the living room.

Fernando had news for Antonio. The Luhan House creeped him out too. He lay his head back on the leather chair and closed his eyes for a moment, seeing a barrage of bright colors popping up against the screen of his mind's eye. The colors faded to black and white, leaving only the image of a photo of Dennis Hopper he'd seen years ago behind the bar at the Taos Inn. Dennis wore a western hat with the sides of the brim rolled up and had a cigarette in his mouth and his eyes half closed. Suddenly Hopper's lips began to move around the cigarette as he spoke: "Come on across, man...free yourself...there's no stress here... no worries...it's groovy, once you get used to the medium...."

Medium?

Sitting by himself in the haunted living room, Fernando fell into his usual brooding. It occurred to him that as you grew older, the more you found yourself living with ghosts. That was especially true for those like him who work or worked in law enforcement, where violence and death were regular occurrences. Over the years he'd become haunted by all the people who'd come to him asking for help—help that he had not always been able to provide. They reminded him of the mistakes he'd made, the things he should or should not have done, the regrets and the guilt that never goes away. Not to mention close friends his age who had passed: Fidel Rodriguez, Raoul Garcia, Wayne Fontenot, and so many others. Ghosts now, they were still with him, following him everywhere. His entire generation was passing before his eyes. He'd lived long enough to find himself surrounded by ghosts.

The more he brooded, the more he realized that it was not so surprising that Jack Lacy had come back to Taos chasing the ghost of Dennis Hopper. Just another member of his generation surrounded by ghosts.

Moments later one of the staff came walking through the living room, his body pulsating. His shape changed as he walked—skinny one moment, fat the next; tall one moment, short the next. The pulsating man stopped when he spotted Fernando sitting by the fireplace. "Would you like me to build a fire?" he asked, motioning toward the fireplace.

Fernando looked up at him, an older man with gray stubble and short gray hair that seemed to grow longer as they talked. He wore an untucked flannel shirt over jeans that somehow reminded Fernando of pajamas. He seemed eager to please, as did all of the staff here. He had to give them credit.

"Thanks, but I don't think that's necessary, do you?" Fernando said, trying to focus on the here and now. What was the question...a fire? "No...It's not quite cold enough."

"Suit yourself," the man said and walked off.

Fernando sat by himself in the empty living room staring at a cold fireplace and hearing voices from Mabel's bedroom above. He wanted to leave but couldn't seem to act on that desire. He wondered how he was going to get out of this chair, let alone the Luhan House.

6

Later, after he heard Antonio wander off somewhere in the house talking to himself, Fernando opened his eyes and tried to meditate by focusing on a Navajo rug hanging on the wall over the fireplace. His body began to relax and the visions began to fade. He hadn't had a chance to unwind all day. Too much racing around after Jack Lacy. One thing after another. His eyelids began to feel heavy. Finally he closed them and tried to blot out everything that had happened over the past twenty-four hours. Let it go, breathe deeply, relax....

The ringing of his cell phone brought him back to consciousness. Where was he? Then he remembered, the Mabel Dodge Luhan House with Antonio and Lacy. They were in Taos to send Lacy off to the Happy Hunting Ground. The sooner the better.

Fernando fumbled for his phone, trying to pull it out of his shirt pocket, but the damn thing slipped through his fingers and fell on the rug under his chair. By the time he picked it up the ringing had stopped. Still feeling groggy, he held the phone in his lap for a few minutes to clear his head. When he saw the call was from Manny, he clicked on the number and returned the call.

"Hi Fernando," Manny said immediately. He sounded deflated, not his usual happy go lucky self. "I'm calling to ask you some questions about the John Hammond killing...and I need you to be honest with me, okay? This is a big deal down here, as you should know. In spite of his recent drinking and deviant behavior, Hammond was a public figure, someone who had a lot of fans."

"Yeah, okay," Fernando mumbled.

"So far we've done some preliminary investigations," Manny continued. "We talked to Fred Mondragon at La Fonda. Fred said he saw you and Antonio helping Jack Lacy leave La Fonda this morning. So Lacy, the professional assassin who caused us so much trouble last year, was in town for some unknown reason. Forensics has determined the bullet that killed Hammond came from a three-fifty-seven Colt Python, a very expensive pistol. I doubt there are many, if any, Colt Pythons in Santa Fe. You see where I'm going with this?"

Fernando held his tongue. Manny didn't.

"Then we talked to your wife," Manny added. "Estelle said you'd gone up to Taos to help Antonio with a quote unquote 'urgent' matter. I assume that urgent matter is the reappearance of Jack Lacy. So I want you to tell me truthfully what the hell you're doing up in Taos with Jack Lacy and Antonio. Now listen, I know you can talk the rattle off a rattlesnake, but I want the truth, none of your famous circumventions. No bullshit, amigo. What the hell are you doing?"

"I think I'll take the Fifth on that," Fernando said.

"You're not on the fucking witness stand," Manny shot back. "Tell me what you're doing with Jack Lacy, goddamnit!"

Taken aback, Fernando took a deep breath and then another. He decided to fess up...since Manny already knew Lacy had killed Hammond, what difference would it make. "Look ...Lacy's dying. He has Glioblastoma, the burning pit disease, from his time in the Marines during the first Iraq war. He has only weeks, maybe days left. He came back to Taos because he wants to be buried in Jesus Nazareno Cemetery near the grave of Dennis Hopper, an old friend of Lacy's. Antonio and I are helping him make final arrangements. That's the truth—that's all I'm doing up here. I plan to leave as soon as I can...if not sooner!"

"Okay, but why did he shoot John Hammond?" Manny asked.

"Lacy said Hammond grabbed him on the way into La Fonda and wouldn't let go. He was scared."

"Grabbed him? It's hard to believe that a professional assassin would shoot an old man for just grabbing him," Manny replied. "I mean, Lacy is one mean motherfucker. Why would Hammond scare him?"

Fernando sighed. "Lacy has a hair trigger—as you know. And Hammond could be a real asshole—as you also know."

"So where are you staying in Taos?" Manny asked, suddenly changing the subject.

Instead of answering, Fernando clicked off without responding and put away his phone.

Now what? Did Manny's last question mean he was thinking about coming up to Taos? He hoped not. That would complicate the situation even further. He liked Manny, but the little man could be difficult, even petulant at times.

Worried about what Manny would do, Fernando left his comfortable chair in the living room and walked through the office and out of the Luhan House. He was halfway to the Gate House Cottage when he saw Antonio walking toward him.

Antonio waved. "Jack just called—he's done in Mabel's bedroom and wants to go back to the Gate House Cottage."

The two of them walked back into the Luhan House. Once again they climbed the rickety stairs. They found Lacy standing up looking out one of the two big windows abutting Mabel's bed, one on either side. He seemed intent on watching something on the patio below.

"Hey, Jack," Antonio said. He checked his watch. "Are you hungry—you ready for lunch?"

Fernando, surprised, checked his watch. He'd totally lost track of the time. It was, indeed, time for lunch.

Lacy turned to look at them. "I don't eat much."

"Well, I'm starving," Antonio said. "You want us to take you back to the Gate House Cottage, or do you want to come with us? You could at least have some coffee or something light."

Lacy nodded. "Okay. Coffee."

Out of curiosity Fernando approached Lacy. "So did you contact Dennis Hopper?"

Lacy nodded.

"What did he say?"

Lacy grimaced, as though he were in pain. "He told me I would know when to let go and that he would help me cross over when the time came. I felt a weight lift off my shoulders when he said that."

Neither Fernando nor Antonio responded. They positioned themselves on either side of Lacy and helped him down the stairs one step at a time. Lacy fought them every step of the way.

7

A sparse crowd had already assembled in the small, tight dining room. A buffet lunch was spread out on a long center table, where the guests helped themselves and then ate at small tables along the walls. Three elderly couples sat at their separate tables, while a couple of young men, laughing and making a lot of noise, sat at a corner table. The elderly guests all turned their attention away from the youngsters to Lacy, who could barely walk, as the three of them entered the room with Antonio and Fernando on either side of Lacy supporting his weight.

"Wow, in what graveyard did you dig him up?" a blond kid wearing a Los Angeles Lakers jersey asked, trying to be funny. His companion laughed, a big kid with a buzz cut and a UCLA T-shirt.

Antonio turned and scowled at the two punks. Fernando grabbed Antonio's arm and pulled him away, wanting to diffuse the situation before Antonio got angry and physically hurt the loudmouths. When the big man became enraged there was no stopping him—he could break both of them over his knee and toss them over his shoulder. Fernando maneuvered Antonio and Lacy toward a corner table on the opposite side of the room from the two punks. He and Antonio lowered Lacy into a chair and then seated themselves.

For a moment Fernando thought they had dodged a possible messy situation, but the loudmouths continued to spout off. "I'm gagging—he smells like a corpse," the blond kid said, a real comedian. His companion pounded the table laughing, spilling a glass of iced tea on the table.

Instantly Antonio jumped up from the table and charged the loudmouths. He grabbed the blond kid by the throat and lifted him off the floor, smashing him back into the wall behind him. "You need to be taught some manners, kid." Blondie's face turned red, his eyes bulged, and he started to choke.

"Hey! Let him go!" the kid with the UCLA T-shirt pleaded, standing up from their table. He was bigger than the blond kid, but still a good half-foot shorter and a hundred pounds lighter than Antonio.

At that Fernando stood up and began walking toward the other table. He might not be as intimidating as Antonio, but at 180 pounds of solid muscle and an intense try-me attitude, he didn't need to be.

Just then Francis Rose came hurrying into the dining room from the office. "Enough! Stop it! You young fellers get out of here immediately. You started this with your rowdy behavior. Now scoot!"

In response Antonio dropped the blond kid, who fell back heavily on his chair. "Oww!" he howled when he landed. Then the two punks quickly grabbed their cell phones and other gear and headed for the exit. Neither of them said a word as they skedaddled.

Francis turned to her other guests and said, "I apologize for the disturbance. These things happen from time to time. I hope it doesn't disrupt your vacation. We'll keep a close eye on those two."

When he reached the office, the punk with the UCLA T-shirt turned to face them and gave them the finger before exiting the building. He slammed the door hard behind him.

"Could be trouble," Fernando said, wondering if they would hear from the punks again.

"Hah! Don't worry about them," Antonio said, always the optimist. The big man always dismissed threats from others, convinced that he could handle anyone, anywhere, anytime.

After things settled down, Antonio brought Lacy a bowl of chicken rice soup and then went back for his plate, a huge mound of chicken, potatoes, and vegetables. The big man ate like a horse.

Fernando grabbed some chicken and vegetables before Antonio could come back for seconds. Antonio had already taken most of the potatoes.

Lacy took his time, eating only a few spoonfuls of his soup. He grimaced every time he swallowed. Finally he pushed his bowl of soup away and pointed to the window across the room where a beam of sunlight splashed into the room. "Look—do you see them?"

Fernando looked up but saw nothing but sunshine flooding the tiny room. "See what?"

Lacy did not respond.

Antonio mumbled something but didn't look up.

When they finished eating, Antonio helped Lacy walk out to the courtyard while Fernando stayed behind to apologize to Francis for their part in the dining room altercation.

Francis laughed. "I thought your friend—the big guy—might kill one of those unruly youngsters. But don't worry, they deserved to be taught a lesson. We've had worse incidents here."

"Hopefully, it won't happen again," Fernando said.

Outside, Fernando noticed a new bright red Ford Mustang with California license plates parked in the large lot, over toward the Juniper House, a separate building with additional rooms for guests. Fernando connected the dots. The two punks were rich, privileged kids from California. Didn't surprise him, not one bit, given their attitude toward a man who was obviously very sick.

Fortunately the punks were nowhere in sight, so Fernando made his way across the parking lot to the Gate House Cottage. As he approached he saw someone or something in the patio getting up from the wrought iron table. At first he thought it was Antonio, but as the figure turned to face him he saw a much shorter man with long black hair and a headband around his forehead. Fernando paused. Was he still feeling the effects of the peyote? The man looked exactly like Dennis Hopper during his Taos years. Was it one of the grounds crew at the Luhan House...or Dennis Hopper's ghost coming to help Lacy cross over? What?

Fernando ran over to the wall and looked in at the patio, but the figure was gone. Disappeared into thin air, whatever or whoever it was. Suddenly he felt disoriented. Was he losing his grip?

Confused, Fernando walked around to the front door of the Gate House Cottage. He found Antonio and Lacy sitting in the living room. "Did you just see someone in the patio?" he asked, from where he stood in the doorway.

Antonio looked up from the sofa, where he sat reading the Taos News. "No...we haven't seen anyone else. Why?"

"I saw someone just now," Fernando replied.

Antonio put down his newspaper. "What'd he look like?"

Fernando described the figure he'd seen.

"Jesus, that sounds like Dennis Hopper," Antonio said.

Fernando bit his tongue. He didn't know what to say or what to think. He had nothing. No response.

"Well, I have some good news finally," Antonio said, changing the topic. "I finally got through to Maria Sofia Hernandez—she's the Taos curandera I've been trying to reach. Among other things, she helps souls cross over after death. She wants to meet Jack before she agrees to set up a crossover session. She's gonna stop by tomorrow morning at ten o'clock. I also heard back from the caretaker of Jesus Nazareno Cemetery. They'll give Jack a plot close to Dennis Hopper's for a contribution of fifty thousand dollars. They asked if Jack wanted a funeral at the San Francisco de Asis Church down the road, like Dennis had, but I told them that a funeral wouldn't be necessary. Is that right, Jack?"

"What?" Lacy asked, sitting in a large stuffed chair across from the sofa where he had been half asleep.

"You don't want a funeral, right?"

"Hell no, why would I want a funeral now, I'm not dead yet?" Lacy asked, confused.

Antonio threw open his arms. "Never mind."

8

After Lacy finished his nap, they all went outside on the patio for some fresh air. While tolerable, the Gate House Cottage reeked of one hundred years of use and abuse: a combination of dust, mold, and human rot. Sitting at the wrought iron table, Lacy informed Antonio and Fernando that he wanted a local Taos santero to carve a wooden cross for his grave at Jesus Nazareno Cemetery, similar to the carved wooden cross on Dennis Hopper's grave, which was spectacular.

"Shouldn't be a problem," Antonio said. "Lots of santeros in Taos eager for commissions."

"And I don't want any religious inscriptions or symbols on the cross, only my name and dates. If there's room for an inscription, just say, 'He was a soldier who did what he was trained to do.' Nothing else."

Antonio nodded. "I like that. It's simple and distinctive," he said. He took a pen and a piece of paper out of his shirt pocket and handed it to Lacy. "Write down your birth date and the inscription exactly as you want it."

Lacy struggled with the pen but managed to jot down the information and pass the paper back to Antonio.

Just then they heard a car pull up outside the Gate House Cottage, near where their two vehicles were parked. The driver blasted his horn again and again until it became annoying. "Let me handle this," Fernando said, thinking it was the two young punks from California in their red Mustang. He could send them on their way without harming them physically. He hoped.

"Knock it off!" Fernando yelled, bursting out of the front door of the Gate House Cottage. He stopped when he saw the Santa Fe Police cruiser with Manny in the driver's seat. Fucking Manny! He came anyway. Manny was the last person Fernando wanted to see and he suspected he wasn't alone. Antonio and Lacy were liable to get a bit testy when they spotted Manny. More trouble.

Manny opened the door of the cruiser and stepped out quickly, standing there with his arms on his hips staring at Fernando. "I thought you might be here. I stopped first at the Sagebrush Inn and then the El Pueblo Lodge but didn't see your Cherokee. Then I remembered that Lacy considered himself a friend of Dennis Hopper, who owned this place in the seventies. I saw your Cherokee over here by the gate when I pulled into the parking lot."

Fernando sighed. "Why are you here, Manny? Lacy's dying. I already told you this. Leave it alone. Let sleeping dogs die."

Manny had to laugh. "Sleeping dogs die? That's funny, but I already told you that I need to talk to Lacy about what happened that night outside La Fonda—to get his version of why he shot Hammond," Manny replied. "The Chief and the Mayor are both on my ass because they're getting flack from the community activists around town, for whom Hammond was a fucking hero, if not a goddamn saint. They're complaining we haven't done enough to bring John's killer to justice. The community activists are more persistent than the realtors and the Better Business Bureau. You of all people should remember that."

Fernando did remember that—all too well, in fact. As lead detective he'd listened to the Chief's complaints for over ten years. It was even worse if the Mayor and city council and the other organizations got involved.

Fernando threw open his arms. What could he say? "I do remember, but come take a look at Lacy, maybe you'll change your mind."

Manny slammed the door of his cruiser, but before he could walk up to the Gate House Cottage the two young punks from California came striding across the parking lot, having heard the honking earlier. They marched directly up to Manny, completely ignoring Fernando.

"Hey, officer, I want to lodge a complaint against the big fucker who's staying here," the blond punk said. "I want you to arrest him. He assaulted me—tried to choke me to death back in the dining room a few minutes ago. Just take a look at my neck." Here the punk mugged for Manny, leaning his head up and to the side so Manny could see the red line around his neck. "See what he did to me? Tried to kill me."

Manny frowned, turning to Fernando. "What the hell is he talking about— Antonio?"

"Yeah, these two guys were mouthing off in the dining room, referring to Lacy as a corpse and generally being belligerent. Antonio grabbed the kid and taught him some manners."

"Bullshit!" the blond kid shot back. "He tried to kill me. Just ask the old lady at the front desk."

"Her name is Francis," Fernando said "Francis Rose."

"Whatever...I want the big guy arrested."

Now the guy wearing the UCLA shirt stepped forward, almost in Manny's face. "We're armed. We can take care of it ourselves, if you can't." He patted his side, as if he was packing a pistol.

The blond waved his friend back, trying to get him to shut up. He was clearly the brains in this smart-ass duo.

"That would be a big mistake, my friend," Fernando said.

"We know our Second Amendment Rights," the big kid with the UCLA T-shirt said, out of the blue.

"Second Amendment Rights?" Fernando responded.

Frustrated, Manny waved his hands. "Hello! Look, if you really want to pursue this, you'll have to take your story to the Taos police. I have no jurisdiction here. I'm from Santa Fe."

The two punks looked at each other. Then the blond kid turned back to Manny. "You won't help us?"

"Not my jurisdiction. I can't help you," Manny said.

With that the two punks climbed back in their Mustang and screeched off fast, making sure to shower Manny and Fernando with a burst of dirt and sand. A couple of real pricks.

"Privileged little shits from California," Fernando said.

Manny laughed. "They know their Second Amendment Rights. Everyone and his uncle claims to know their Second Amendment Rights. Yet another example of a well-regulated militia, right? How the amendment is interpreted—or misinterpreted—is a fucking joke."

"They could be trouble," Fernando said.

"Not my jurisdiction," Manny said.

9

As they turned and walked up to the Gate House Cottage, they saw Lacy step unsteadily out of the door holding a long-barrel pistol with a silencer on the end. He pointed the pistol straight ahead and said, "Want me to shoot the bastards...are they gone...what....?"

"Put the gun away, Jack," Fernando said. "They're just a couple of punk kids who don't know any better. We don't need any guns."

Lacy deposited his pistol in the deep pocket of his waist coat. Then he happened to notice Manny and the police cruiser. He pointed to Manny. "Who's that? What's a cop doing here?"

Worried that Lacy would reach for his gun again, Fernando did his best to defuse the situation. "That's Manny Alvarez, an old friend of mine from my days on the Santa Fe Police Department. He heard about the shooting at La Fonda yesterday. He just stopped by to talk. Nothing to worry about. Let's go inside and shoot the breeze, what do you say?"

Lacy mumbled something under his breath and shuffled back inside the Gate House Cottage.

Fernando and Manny followed.

Once they were all seated at the wrought iron table on the patio, Antonio went back inside to the kitchen and brought back bottles of Modelo for everyone but Lacy, who declined.

"Thanks, this is just what I need, it's been a crazy day," Manny said. "Good to get out of town for a while."

"I'll drink to that," Fernando said to Manny. "Are you spending the night in Taos?"

"I probably will," Manny replied, taking a long drink from his bottle of Modelo. "If I do, I'll stay at the Sagebrush Inn again. This place gives me the creeps, always has. It reeks of the past—and not in a good way. Bad vibes."

Lacy nodded. "It's the ghosts...I think they might be angry here... some of them anyway."

"Maybe you're right," Manny said. "The Sagebrush Inn has its share of ghosts too, but I don't get the same vibe there—the angry vibe."

No one disagreed with that pronouncement.

"So Jack, I understand that you got involved in some sort of altercation out front of La Fonda late last night," Manny said, directing the conversation. He took a pen and notebook out of his pocket. "Can you tell me what happened? I'm trying to get the Chief off my back."

Lacy shook his head. "I already explained—I was attacked."

"How did it happen? Can you be more specific—give me more details?" Manny asked.

"Soon as I stepped out of my taxi, this old derelict—looked like a homeless bum to me—came up and grabbed me by the arm. He wouldn't let go when I asked him to. Instead he attacked me, like I said."

"And that's why you shot him?" Manny asked.

"Hell yes...wouldn't you have shot him?" Lacy fired back, animated now. "He attacked me first. I was just trying to keep the sonofabitch away from me before he could hurt me."

"So it was self-defense then?" Manny replied, eager to find a way to placate the Chief as well as his friends at the table.

"That's it...self defense...exactly!" Lacy said.

"Okay, I can work with that," Manny said. "It was late and dark on the street that night and you were just trying to get to your hotel room after a long day of traveling when this guy looking like a dangerous street person approached and attacked you physically. You told the guy to leave you alone, and when he didn't you shot him in self defense to save your life. What else could you have done, given that you were all alone out there with a dangerous derelict?"

"Damn right!" Lacy said.

Manny nodded. He put away his pen and notebook and stared at Lacy. Speaking softly now, he asked, "How much time do you have, Jack?"

"I don't," Lacy replied. "Doc gave me six months to live. That was eight months ago. I'm living on borrowed time."

That silenced the table. Manny, Antonio and Fernando nursed their beers, while Lacy's eyelids grew heavy and his head began to droop.

No one at the table spoke until Lacy suddenly struggled up out of his chair and said, "I'm gonna take a nap—I can't keep up with you youngsters anymore." He walked into the master bedroom and lay down on the big bed.

When Lacy was safely out of the room, Manny turned to Antonio and asked, "What exactly are you doing for him up here?"

Antonio lowered his usually booming voice. "I'm helping him leave, basically. I promised him I'd be with him at the end. He wants to be buried in Jesus Nazareno Cemetery as close as possible to Dennis Hopper's grave. I managed to get him a plot, even though he has no connection to Taos. I had to make a large contribution in Jack's name to the cemetery. Jack opened a joint checking account for us and deposited five hundred thousand dollars so I would be able to play for expenses like this. He's also hiring—if that's the right word—a curandera named Maria Sofia Hernandez who specializes in helping dying people cross over to the spirit world. Maria Sofia Hernandez is her name, but she goes by Luz, just Luz. She's coming to meet him tomorrow morning to see if she's able to help him. She hasn't said how much the crossover ceremony will cost. I guess we'll find out tomorrow."

"Luz?" Manny asked.

"Yeah, Spanish for light," Antonio replied. "I guess because she helps her patients go into the light."

"So Lacy has a lot of money?" Manny asked, again changing the topic of conversation.

Antonio shrugged. "I don't know. He spends money lavishly, so my guess is that he doesn't have as much as he wants people to believe. Not millions anyway. More like a few hundred thousand."

"So then you intend to hang with Lacy until he dies. That's what I hear you saying?"

Antonio nodded.

Manny checked his watch. "Well, I think I will stay at the Sagebrush Inn tonight. Fuck the Chief. He'll get his report tomorrow. I better get over there and book a room in the new building. That's the only building I can stand. Rooms in the other buildings are shit-holes."

Manny finished his Modelo quickly and then stood up and headed for the patio gate. Fernando followed Manny, while Antonio went into the master bedroom to check on Lacy.

Fernando grabbed Manny as he opened the door of his cruiser. "So what will you tell the Chief?"

Manny laughed. "That John Hammond was shot and killed by a dead man. You can't very well arrest a dead man."

"No, seriously, what will you tell him?" Fernando repeated.

"I'll tell him just what Lacy said, that Hammond attacked him physically as soon as he stepped out of the taxi and that he had to fire in self defense, as simple as that," Manny said. "I'll finesse it a bit, add more details about Hammond's aggressive behavior and the threat he posed to a very sick man all alone on the dark street, an honored veteran who was dying from Glioblastoma. Make my report all about self-defense. Shouldn't be a problem."

"Good," Fernando said, "because he's in no condition to be jailed. He can hardly walk."

"So I saw. Makes no sense to arrest and charge a man who's on his death bed. How long do you think he has?" Manny asked.

"Not long. He wants the curandera to orchestrate his crossover, however that works. I'll find out more tomorrow."

"Okay, why don't you and Antonio meet me for dinner later at the Sagebrush Inn—Lacy too if he wants to come," Manny said. "They have great food, as you know. How about we meet on their patio about six o'clock? That'll give me a little time to put together some notes for my report on the Hammond shooting. Give me a head start, because I know the Chief will start bugging me as soon as I walk into the station tomorrow."

"Sounds good," Fernando said. "We'll meet you on the patio at six. At least I'll be there, even if I can't get Antonio and Lacy."

Manny saluted and climbed into his cruiser. In contrast to the two punks in the Mustang, Manny drove off slowly, turning onto Morada Lane and disappearing behind the tree-line.

A thought occurred to Fernando as he watched Manny drive away. Maybe he should stay at the Sagebrush Inn with Manny. He might be more comfortable at the Sagebrush Inn. After all, the ghosts were friendlier there. Or so he and everyone else thought.

10

Instead of riding with Antonio, Fernando decided to drive his Cherokee to the Sagebrush Inn for dinner. He left earlier, wanting to stop by the Taos Plaza to see what was shaking down there. He had lots of fond memories of Taos, especially when he was single and would come up with friends to hang around the bars looking for action. His wild years. Remembering some of their escapades embarrassed him, and yet if he could go back he wouldn't change one damn thing. In fact, he wouldn't change anything about his past. Nothing.

Since he had his own wheels, he could spend the night at the Sagebrush Inn or go back to the Gate House Cottage. His travel duffle was still in the rear compartment of the Cherokee waiting his decision. He parked on the Plaza and walked around the square once and then up to Martyrs Restaurant, to make sure it was still there just in case he decided to stay in Taos. It was, so he climbed back in the Cherokee and headed for the Sagebrush Inn. Even in late October the highway, called Paseo del Pueblo Sur on this side of the Taos Plaza, was crowded with tourists looking for a place to stay for the night. Like Santa Fe, Taos had become a tourist town.

When Fernando turned into the drive of the Sagebrush Inn he saw Manny's cruiser parked in front of the new building, where the Sagebrush reception desk was located. He drove on by the cruiser and parked across the lot, next to the outdoor patio. This way he could enter through the patio gate and not the front entrance. Just easier, in case he had to make a quick exit, for whatever reason.

As soon as he climbed out of his Cherokee he spotted Antonio and Manny sitting at one of the tables. Lacy must have decided not to come. The man in black couldn't have died in the forty or fifty minutes since Fernando had left the Gate House Cottage. If he had, Antonio and Manny certainly wouldn't be sitting on the Sagebrush patio with smiles on their faces and beers in their hands.

Fernando opened the patio gate and walked over to the festive table. "No Lacy, eh?" he asked, taking a seat at the table.

"He didn't want to come, as I expected," Antonio said. "He had me get him some soup from the dining room. That's about all he eats anymore—soup, and he barely eats any of that."

Manny raised his glass of beer. "Cheers! It's good to get away from the old bastard. What a change since the last time he was here. You must be getting tired of taking care of him."

Antonio shrugged. "I owe him that. He saved my ass in Iraq on several occasions."

While they talked, a spritely young woman in jeans and a white Guatemalan embroidered shirt came over to their table. "Can I bring you something to drink?" she asked Fernando with a big smile on her face.

"Modelo draft, please!" Fernando said emphatically, realizing after the fact that he must have sounded downright desperate.

"Make that three—we're running low," Antonio added.

When the young server returned with their drinks, she took their dinner orders. Fernando ordered what he always ordered: chicken enchiladas with red chile. Antonio ordered what he always ordered: a combination plate, one of everything imaginable. Manny surprised them by ordering the breakfast burrito, which at the Sagebrush Inn was available all day, every day.

Beer number two loosened Manny's tongue. Halfway through the beer he sat back in his chair and frowned at Antonio. "You know, I have to ask you guys. Don't get pissed, but why do you give a good goddamn about Jack Lacy, who's nothing but a cold-blooded killer? You know this, both of you, because you've seen him in action. He kills people for a living. He's a fucking assassin, remember? A criminal! You treat him like he's some kind of hero, a kind old man who's been a good Samaritan all his life. But he's not, he's a cold-blooded killer."

Fernando raised his hands in defense. "Not me. I'm not interested in taking care of him. I agree with what you're saying, but in terms of the Hammond killing, I just don't think it makes any sense to go through all the trouble arresting and charging a man who's gonna be dead in a few days. It seems like a waste of resources. Why bother wasting your time on a dead man?"

"Justice, that's why!" Manny fired back. "So Santa Feans can be rest-assured that we will arrest and prosecute anyone guilty of killing another human being. Let him die in custody, where he belongs."

Antonio interrupted Manny, getting angry now. "Easy for you to say, but I can't be objective, okay? He's my friend, my war buddy. You're a fucking loner, so how would you know?"

This went on until their food arrived, at which time they took a short break to eat and then resumed arguing about Jack Lacy over more beers. Too many beers, as it turned out.

Manny was the first to fall. "Jesus, I can't keep up with you guys. I'm smashed. Need to walk back to my room." He took a fifty-dollar bill out of his wallet and tossed it on the table.

Fernando and Antonio watched Manny walk unsteadily across the parking lot to the new building, where he fumbled with his key card for a couple of minutes before managing to open the door.

Antonio waved dismissively at Manny. "These young people can't hold their liquor."

"Well, be that as it may, I guess I'm staying with you at the Gate House Cottage again tonight," Fernando said. "I don't have enough energy—or clarity of mind—to go book a room here."

Antonio ignored Fernando and waved the young server over. "One more round for the road."

She gave them a hard stare of disapproval and then said, "Are you guys sure you want another beer?"

"Of course I'm sure!" Antonio replied, raising his voice.

The server scurried off before Antonio could get out of his chair and create a scene. She returned a few minutes later with the two beers, which she set delicately on the table and then disappeared.

They drank their last beers without talking, enjoying the cool night air and the stars twinkling in the clear New Mexico sky. A half moon hung in the sky over Ranchos de Taos.

"Okay, it's time. I better head back to the Gate House Cottage to check on Jack," Antonio said with a sigh. "To tell you the truth, I am sick of taking care of him, but I told him I would be with him at the end and now I don't know how to get out of it. You know what I mean?"

"I do," Fernando said. "Happens to me all the time. I'll agree to do something for someone and then later wonder what I was thinking— why in hell did I ever agree to do that?"

Antonio nodded. "Yeah, well, I hate to admit it, but sometimes when I go out I find myself hoping Jack will be dead in the room when I return...just to put an end to it. That I'll walk in and find him gone."

"If and when that happens, do you have a funeral parlor in Taos to call?" Fernando asked.

Antonio nodded. "Already contacted and paid for. They're waiting, like the rest of us...including Jack. I think that's all Jack wants now...to cross over...to join Dennis Hopper."

"So he says," Fernando said, trying not to be sarcastic. "Apparently Jack has been talking to Dennis Hopper, who's gonna be waiting for him on the other side."

Antonio smiled. "Who knows, maybe he can talk to Hopper. Maybe he's on that same frequency now that he's dying."

"Or maybe he's delusional," Fernando said, swigging the last of his beer.

11

Voices woke Fernando in the middle of the night. Whispers as soft as dreams. It took him a few moments to get his bearings. The pieces of the puzzle came together slowly in his mind. Finally he remembered: he was sleeping on a sofa in the Gate House Cottage with Antonio and Lacy after a night of heavy drinking at the Sagebrush Inn. Groggy, his head throbbed when he tried to open his eyes and listen to the voices. Were they calling him? What did they want?

Darkness enclosed the room. The only light came from a small window across the room, where moonlight created a faint halo around the window frame. Fernando eased his legs off the sofa and sat up, his head pounding and his back aching from sleeping on the lumpy sofa. Big mistake. He should have stayed at the Sagebrush Inn last night, even if he had to pay for his own room. The first time he tried to stand up he lost his balance and fell back on the sofa. He sat for a few seconds before trying again. This time he held on to the arm of the sofa until he got his balance.

The voices called to him again from somewhere in the rear of the house. Whispers really, because he couldn't make out what they were saying. He stumbled forward, making his way through the darkness toward the master bedroom. He stifled a yelp when he collided with a small table along the wall, hurting his hip. Worrying about the noise, he paused a few moments to see if the voices stopped. They didn't, so he pushed forward into a dark hallway that led to the master bedroom where Lacy slept next to the French doors opening to the patio.

As he walked further down the hallway Fernando could see the master bedroom, where a small lamp on the bed-stand illuminated an empty bed. No Lacy! The dying man must have gotten out of bed. To go where? The light in the adjoining bathroom had not been turned on, so where was Lacy? Outside?

When Fernando heard voices coming from the patio he knew where to find the dying man. He crept over to the wide-open French doors that looked out on the dark patio. From the doorway he saw a half moon drooping low in the western sky with its feeble rays dissolving in the darkness of the patio. Sitting at the table wearing a robe was Lacy, who appeared to be speaking to someone sitting across the wrought iron table. Did someone enter the house or patio while he was sleeping? Or could Lacy be talking to himself...or to something more ethereal?

Fernando eased out onto the patio, staying back against the wall. He craned his neck to get a look at whomever Lacy was talking with at the table. All he saw across from Lacy was a black object, a shadow among the shadows, silhouetted by the moon's rays that seemed to make the object glimmer.

"She will...she'll take me to the light," Lacy said, hardly more than a whisper. "So if you meet me on the other side...."

Suddenly Fernando heard footsteps coming through the bedroom toward the French doors, followed by the sound of something shattering inside the bedroom. Sounded like a lamp. "Fuck!" Antonio cursed. Then the big man burst, almost falling, through the French doors and asked, "What's going on out here?"

Instantly the glimmering object dissolved into the darkness. Gone with the snap of the fingers.

Antonio noticed Fernando against the wall and edged closer. "Who's he talking to?"

"I have no idea," Fernando said. "Himself?"

Without replying, Antonio hurried over to the table. "Hey Jack— what's happening? Are you okay?"

Lacy turned to face Antonio, moonlight glancing off his face. "Leave me alone...you interrupted...something very important...now I'll have to contact him again...I'm getting so tired I...wish I could just go with him now...leave me alone...I need to rest before...."

With that Lacy laid his head on the table and appeared to fall asleep, almost instantly.

"Is he dead?" Fernando asked.

"No, he's still breathing," Antonio said. "Should we try to move him back inside."

"No, leave him alone, just like he said," Fernando replied. "Let him continue to do whatever he was doing. He's dying, for God's sake. He should be able to do what he wants."

Without responding, Antonio moved slowly away from the table, joining Fernando.

"You think he was talking to Dennis?" Antonio asked.

"I suppose...he was asking someone or something to meet him on the other side," Fernando said. "Who else would it be?"

Antonio sighed. "I wish this would just be over with."

"It'll be over soon. You can tell by looking into his eyes. He's a dead man walking. I'll give him a day or two, that's all."

"He'll be happy when it's finally over," Antonio said. "That's the only thing he wants now."

"The sooner the better," Fernando replied. As soon as he said it, he realized how callous he'd sounded.

Antonio did not respond. He watched Lacy sleeping at the table for a while and then said, "Well, shit! I suppose I better stay with him." Then he made his way his way to the table and took a seat next to Lacy.

Shaking his head at Antonio's loyalty, Fernando turned and went back into the master bedroom. He switched on a light so he could find his way back to the sofa in the living room. Exhausted and hung over, he sprawled on the sofa and pulled up the lone blanket Antonio had given him after finding it in one of the back closets. He knew he should find his duffle bag and take a Tylenol for his headache, but he felt too damned tired. He just couldn't work up the energy to fetch the duffle bag, which he'd left in the Cherokee.

He tried to sleep, but every time he closed his eyes he saw the image of Dennis Hopper with long hair and headband that had been haunting him. He couldn't get the image out of his mind. He began to wonder if Hopper was trying to contact him too, as well as Lucy.

But why? He wasn't even sure if he believed in such things.

It wasn't his time to cross over, was it?

12

Once again voices woke Fernando. This time the room was flooded with light when he cracked open his eyes. His headache had subsided, but his throat felt as dry as the desert sand. Antonio stood off to the side of the sofa talking loudly to someone on his cell phone. The big man clicked off just as Fernando sat up and tossed his blanket on a nearby coffee table. He'd slept all night in his clothes, but at least he'd taken off his hiking boots. He found them under the coffee table and put them on, starting to wake up finally.

"Damn, do you know how you toss and turn in your sleep? I heard you all night long," Antonio said. "Do you ever get any sleep?"

"So I'm told," Fernando croaked, the best he could do with a parched throat. "Estelle says the same thing."

"I just got off the phone with Luz, the curandera," Antonio said. "She'll be here this morning before noon, probably sometime between nine and ten our time. She said she couldn't be more specific because she doesn't 'follow' the clock. Whatever that means."

"Maybe she follows the sun," Fernando mumbled.

Antonio gave him a dirty look.

"I desperately need some water," Fernando said, as he got to his feet and headed for the kitchen. He grabbed a glass in the cupboard and drank down two full glasses of water, which made his abused throat feel somewhat better. For the thousandth time he swore to himself that he would never drink alcohol again. He wondered how Manny fared last night after staggering to his room at the Sagebrush Inn. Couldn't be any worse than he felt this morning.

Antonio followed him into the small kitchen, complete with stove, refrigerator and an ancient countertop. Looked like the appliances hadn't been used in a very long time. "I made myself a cup of coffee earlier.

The cheap bastards only left two cartridges for the Keurig, but I saved you one of them. That took a lot of willpower, so you owe me bigtime."

"Two? Jesus, I need a pot of coffee," Fernando replied.

"Here, let me make you a cup," Antonio said, filling a cup with water and then brewing Fernando a cup.

Fernando took a long drink of coffee, not bothering to look for the milk and sugar he usually added. "You never have a hangover. How can you drink so much without getting a hangover?"

Antonio laughed. "What do you think? I weigh over two hundred and eighty pounds."

Fernando looked in the empty refrigerator and moaned. "Sorry, but I need something to eat, a real breakfast. I'm going over to the dining room. You want me to bring you more coffee?"

"Yeah...and grab a croissant or something," Antonio replied. "Anything I can eat by hand."

Fernando finished his cup of coffee and walked over to the dining room. One elderly couple sat at the first table. Otherwise the room was empty. He thought he might grab two pastries and coffees to go, but when he saw the hot trays of scrambled eggs and sausage, he changed his mind. He filled a plate with the steaming hot food and grabbed a donut for dessert. He gobbled the food quickly, drinking two more cups of coffee in the process. After he finished eating, he prepared a coffee to go and grabbed a donut for Antonio.

On the way out he brushed past the two young punks who'd caused a scene yesterday. Or rather, they brushed past him. The blond kid bumped his shoulder on purpose, making Fernando spill the coffee he carried.

"Hey—watch it!" Fernando said.

"Piss off!" the big one replied, still wearing his UCLA T-shirt.

Fernando had a notion to set down the coffee and donut and teach the big mouth a lesson in manners but decided against it. Antonio was waiting for more coffee and his finger food.

Back at the Gate House Cottage he found Antonio sitting in the master bedroom watching Lacy, who sat in the bed propped up by pillows behind and around him. The emaciated little man seemed to be sleeping, eyes closed and mouth open. He made gurgling sounds as he snored.

"Thanks," Antonio said, taking the coffee and donut.

"Sorry, the cup's only half full," Fernando said. "I encountered the two punks from California on the way out of the dining room. They gave me the cold shoulder. Literally."

Antonio muttered a string of profanities but eagerly accepted the coffee and donut.

Fernando wandered over to the bed where Lacy lay. With his eyes closed and his emaciated body, Lacy looked dead already. Fernando had to look closely to see Lacy's chest rising and falling ever so slightly. The life force, or whatever you wanted to call it, was ebbing in Lacy's shriveled body.

"He goes in and out of consciousness," Antonio said. "I think the end is near. Good thing Luz is coming this morning."

To get away from the death watch Fernando took his cell phone out to the table on the patio. He debated whether to head back to Santa Fe this morning. What else could he do here? He had no idea what Antonio expected of him.

A few minutes later, when the sun was rising high over the patio, his cell phone pinged. He clicked on the message icon and found a text from Estelle. "Where are you? When will you be coming home?"

Feeling guilty for not contacting her earlier, he responded: "Hopefully today, tomorrow at the latest. I'm staying at the Mabel Dodge Luhan House with Antonio. All goes well."

All goes well? He didn't know about that last statement, but he didn't want Estelle to worry.

Not long after that he heard a car driving across the parking lot and stopping outside the Gate House Cottage. Must be Luz, the curandera, he figured. Two car doors opened and closed outside. Then he heard talking in the living room. He walked inside the cottage to find Antonio talking to a stout, big-boned woman with long curly black hair to the middle of her back. Dressed in a long purple dress under a lacy purple shawl, she wore a cross and a large pendant necklace with stars, animals, and Zodiac signs dangling from a silver chain. Fernando felt her presence as he walked into the room. She had an aura of strength around her that was palpable. You could feel it. He'd encountered few—very few—people who had that power.

Behind her stood a tough-looking short man in jeans and a black leather jacket. He looked like some kind of bodyguard, the way he stood off a ways behind her like a statue, waiting.

"Greetings," Luz said to Fernando. "I'm called Luz and this is my brother Daniel. He comes with me when I meet someone new...to help keep me safe." She smiled broadly, with the implication that she didn't need anybody to keep her safe.

Daniel nodded but didn't speak.

Luz looked around the room. "Very nice. I've always loved the Luhan House. It's haunted, you know. You can feel the presence of Mabel and Tony and so many of the people who lived here."

"So we've discovered," Fernando said. "Including Dennis Hopper, who was a friend of Lacy's."

Luz regarded Fernando carefully, critically. Sizing him up. "Especially Dennis Hopper," she said. "He was truly larger than life. Not even Mabel had the magnetism or the presence of Dennis Hopper."

"So I understand," Fernando replied.

"Where is Mister Lacy?" Luz asked.

Antonio motioned toward the bedroom. "This way."

Luz and Daniel followed Antonio, while Fernando brought up the rear. He wanted to stay out of the way and out of the conversation. He had no desire to participate in a crossover ceremony. What he really wanted was to disentangle completely and get back to Santa Fe.

"Oh...you're here finally...." Lacy croaked when he saw Luz walk into the bedroom.

"Yes, I am here to assist you," Luz said. Then she turned to Antonio. "I should tell you that the crossover ceremony is rather expensive."

"Not to worry...no problem," Lacy responded, opening his eyes wide. "I'm a millionaire...lots of money."

When Lacy said this, Antonio glanced back at Fernando. Not a good idea to broadcast your wealth to someone you just met, someone as unconventional as Luz. Not to mention her silent, less than friendly brother, who seemed to perk up at the mention of the word 'millionaire.'

"We'll take care of it," Antonio said, staring at Luz's brother. Daniel stared right back.

"Okay, then, I need to visit with Mister Lacy alone, so could the two of you wait outside in the patio please?" Luz asked. "It won't take us long to get to know one another. Maybe fifteen or thirty minutes."

"Get to know one another?" Antonio asked.

"Yes, to see if we can work together, you see," Luz replied. "Some people are resistant—it's difficult, if not impossible to work with them."

Antonio didn't like what he'd just heard. He glanced at Fernando as if he were asking for help. None came. "I guess," he said finally. "I think you'll find Jack eager to work with you."

Fernando followed Antonio outside to the patio, where they sat at the wrought iron table. They noticed that Daniel stayed in the room with Luz, so in fact she was not alone in the room with Lacy. Luz closed the French doors behind them, cutting them out of the meeting altogether.

Antonio sighed. "I don't like this...or Daniel."

"Who said you had to like it?" Fernando replied.

"I mean I don't trust them," Antonio said, giving Fernando the Evil Eye.

"That makes two of us," Fernando said.

13

While waiting impatiently on the patio, Fernando checked his cell phone for texts from Estelle. He found nothing. She hadn't bothered to respond to the text he'd sent earlier. That meant big trouble for him. He knew from experience that silence was a more dangerous sign than anger, at least from Estelle. The longer she waited to respond, the more he had to fear from her response.

After about a half hour of waiting Antonio became agitated. He jumped up from the table and started pacing back and forth on the patio mumbling to himself. One end of the patio to the other. Nonstop.

Antonio's walking back and forth started to irritate Fernando. Finally it drove him crazy. "Why are you so nervous?" Fernando asked. "Are you worried about Luz? Where did you find her anyway?"

Antonio stopped pacing. He turned and frowned at Fernando. "Online, where do you think I found her? She has a professional looking website with lots of flattering recommendations posted there. Luz teaches classes at the Taos branch of the University of New Mexico. She teaches in the Holistic Health and Healing Arts Certificate Program at the Taos campus. So how could she not be legit? She's a college professor, for God's sake?"

Fernando nodded. "Yeah, I'm familiar with that program. In that case I wouldn't worry about it. She must be legit if she teaches at UNM."

In last year's Witchcraft Murders case he'd encountered a young woman named Melissa Vigil who happened to be the girlfriend of the wannabe witch who became a mass murderer. After disentangling herself from her boyfriend, Melissa had moved to Taos and entered the Holistic Health and Healing Arts Certificate Program wanting to be a naturopathic healer. He'd checked out the program and found it impressive, even though personally he wasn't a big fan of holistic healing arts. He preferred traditional medicine.

A few minutes later the French doors opened and a smiling Luz stepped out on the patio, like a ray of sunshine. "We're finished," she announced proudly. "Yes, I think I can help Mister Lacy. I will need some time to prepare my therapy room for the crossover ceremony, but I don't want to wait too long because he is very near the crossover moment now. Why don't you bring him to my home later this afternoon—say about three o'clock?" She reached into one of her many pockets and pulled out a business card that listed her address, complete with a map showing how to get there, and then handed the card to Antonio.

Luz held Antonio's hand for a brief moment. She gave it a gentle squeeze and then let go, smiling.

Antonio glanced at the card and nodded. He seemed incredibly relieved, as if she'd assuaged his concerns by her friendly, nurturing behavior. "Okay, we'll be there at three o'clock then."

"Excellent," Luz said, as she walked back inside the bedroom, where Lacy was still propped up in his bed with a faint smile on his face. He looked weaker than ever, as if it took all of his energy even to sit up. Death was advancing.

"See you soon," she said to Lacy.

Fernando and Antonio watched Luz walk out of the Gate House Cottage. Daniel had disappeared earlier. They had no idea what had become of him.

They went back to the bedroom to check on Lacy and found him asleep. He looked very frail.

"Do you think we should bring him some breakfast...or soup, if they have an early lunch?" Fernando asked.

Antonio threw up his arms. "I don't know. Maybe some soup later, if he's awake and able to eat."

"So what do you want to do now?" Fernando asked. He'd hoped to return to Santa Fe today, maybe after they delivered Lacy to Luz for the crossover ceremony, but that seemed more tenuous by the hour. "What do you think, do you need me to come along when you to take Lacy to Luz? Or would I just be in the way? I'd like to head back to Santa Fe if you don't need me."

Antonio patted Fernando on the back. "No, you wouldn't be in the way. I would really appreciate your company. I don't trust that Daniel character. Something about him. Bad vibes."

Just then Antonio's cell phone rang. Antonio checked the name on the screen and then said to Fernando, "It's the guy from Jesus Nazareno Cemetery. I got in touch with him yesterday."

Antonio sat on the sofa to take the call. After listening for a few seconds, he said, "Okay, that sounds perfect. I would like to see the plot. If you're at the cemetery now, why don't I come over and take a look? I can be there in fifteen minutes. Okay. I'm on my way."

Antonio turned to Fernando. "That was Johnny Espinosa, about the plot in Jesus Nazareno Cemetery. He found one close to Dennis Hopper's grave, like we discussed. He'll show it to us now."

Us? Sounded like he was included. Fernando resigned himself to being part of the graveyard detail.

"You want to drive, or should I?" Antonio asked.

"Why don't you drive," Fernando replied.

After checking on Lacy, they left the Gate House Cottage and climbed into Antonio's Wrangler. On their way out of the parking lot they passed by the two punks who were walking to the big house.

The big guy, still wearing his UCLA T-shirt, gave them the finger and mouthed "fuck you."

Antonio returned the insult. "I'd love to get a chance to teach that little fucker a lesson."

"Just don't kill him, whatever you do, okay?" Fernando said, having seen the damage Antonio could inflict on a human body.

They drove out Morada Lane to Paseo del Pueblo Sur and followed it south past the Sagebrush Inn.

Approaching Ranchos de Taos, Antonio turned left onto Highway 518 and drove down the old two-lane highway. Minutes later he turned left again into the unpaved parking lot of Jesus Nazareno Cemetery and pulled up beside a Toyota Tacoma pick-up. Surrounded by a wire fence, Jesus Nazareno was overrun by weeds and colorful wildflowers, a tumbledown collection of stone markers and hand-carved wooden crosses, backgrounded by the deep blue Taos mountains to the north and west. It was so untended and *au naturel*, not to mention starkly beautiful, that it took your breath away every time you saw it. Fernando and Antonio had been here before, when they had taken Lacy to see Dennis Hopper's grave during the Santa Fe Assassin case. Back when Lacy was still healthy and a very dangerous man.

Fernando's reaction was the same as before. Jesus Nazareno might be the most beautiful cemetery he'd ever seen, except maybe Truchas.

He wondered if he could convince Estelle to buy two plots here. He figured he could get around the residency requirement if he really tried.

They climbed out of the Wrangler and looked for Johnny Espinosa. "There he is," Antonio said, pointing to a small man wearing a baseball cap in the middle of the cemetery. Espinosa waved at them.

Fernando followed Antonio. They walked through an opening in the fence on a dirt path, free from weeds. Off to their right they passed by a wooden ramada under which a statue of Jesus knelt on the ground struggling with his heavy wooden cross. Jesus wore a crown of thorns, with streaks of red blood sliding down his delicately painted face, flesh-colored with a black beard and dark, penetrating eyes. Blue and white flowers, real and artificial, were scattered around the statue. Looked like someone had been here recently bringing flowers.

They walked down the narrow path to Dennis Hopper's grave, where a beautifully carved wooden cross had been erected on a mound of dirt and rock. Headbands and scarves of all colors had been placed on the wooden cross by Hopper's fans, remembering the actor's role in his most famous movie, *Easy Rider*, parts of it filmed nearby in Taos, where Hopper lived during the 1970s after buying the Mabel Dodge Luhan House. Several people had brought bouquets of bright flowers and someone had tucked a leather pouch into an American flag placed next to the wooden cross. An empty whiskey bottle, two full cans of Coors beer, a browned, much-used bong, and several joints completed the graveside décor. Seemed perfect for Hopper. Only thing missing would be a loaded pistol to recapture the many times Hopper ran afoul of the law while in Taos and northern New Mexico.

The words engraved in the wooden cross read: "Dennis Lee Hopper, Born 5-17-36, Died 5-29-10."

"Howdy," Antonio said to Espinosa as they approached a grassy area on the trail. "Thanks for showing us the plot."

"My pleasure," Espinosa said, a small friendly man with a weathered face under his baseball cap. In addition to the cap, he wore jeans, a western shirt, and cowboy boots. "I think this is the closest available plot to Dennis Hopper's grave. It's nice, because there's no rocks, only grass. I can give you the name of a *santero* who can carve a wooden cross like Hopper's."

"Thanks, I appreciate all you're doing," Antonio said. "My friend

Jack Lacy will be pleased. He's an old friend of Dennis Hopper's and really wants to be buried here close to Dennis."

Espinosa smiled, a twinkle in his eye. "I hope your friend is ready for party central. This may be a cemetery, but lotta party animals come to see Dennis Hopper's grave. They bring bottles of whiskey and beer, even drugs, and party right here in the cemetery. Sometimes they pour alcohol on Hopper's grave, you know, to give him a taste. They bring everything. Sometimes even loud music. You should see the people dancing in the aisles!"

"Almost loud enough to raise the dead, eh?" Antonio quipped.

Espinosa laughed. "Yeah, everybody loves Dennis now that he's dead. Not so much when he was alive and living here. He and all his druggie friends had lotta run-ins with the locals, even some with the law."

"So I understand," Antonio said. "He was a wild man, all right. Still hard for me to believe he lived in Taos as long as he did."

Fernando couldn't restrain himself. He stepped forward and asked the question he'd been waiting to ask ever since he'd first seen the cemetery: "Do you ever get reports of people seeing Hopper's ghost here at the cemetery?"

A shadow came across Espinosa's face. His friendly tone became more serious. "Well, I shouldn't probably talk about this, but yes, we hear stories all the time about people seeing Dennis or his ghost here. Some claim to see Dennis smoking the marijuana people leave for him on his grave. Others say they see him weeping with Jesus over at the entrance to the cemetery. Or sometimes walking on the mesa talking to himself. Lotta stories, you know. Hard to keep track of them all."

"Do you believe any of them?" Fernando asked.

Espinosa didn't answer at first. He looked around the cemetery as if making sure no one was around to hear him. "Lotta people here don't like him—never did. Some people think he's the Devil. You gotta be careful what you say. So yes, I believe the stories. Some of them, anyway."

"Some of them," Fernando repeated.

"Well, we won't keep you," Antonio said, cutting off their conversation intentionally, or so it seemed to Fernando. "This plot is fine. I'll put a check in the mail tomorrow unless you want me to bring it to you. I guess the funeral home will take care of the burial details."

Espinosa nodded. "Mail is fine."

Fernando saluted as he walked by Dennis Hopper's grave. He had no idea why he saluted, but it seemed appropriate at the time.

As they climbed back into Antonio's Wrangler, they noticed that Espinosa hadn't moved from where he stood in the cemetery. He stood watching them leave. As if he were somehow suspicious of their intentions.

Antonio fired up the Wrangler and headed back to the Luhan House. Neither one of them spoke on the drive back. Antonio parked near the Gate House Cottage and ran into the house to check on Lacy, while Fernando stayed in the Wrangler for a few minutes brooding about what Espinosa had said about Dennis Hopper and Jesus Nazareno becoming party central for Dennis Hopper's fans, who were by all accounts a notoriously rowdy lot.

Espinosa was right about Dennis Hopper not being liked in Taos by a lot of people, especially the old Hispanic community. Hopper was an outsider, a hell-raiser from Hollywood, whose lifestyle was not only foreign but often insulting to local values. Yet ironically in spite of the prevailing attitude toward him, Hopper had returned in death. He'd chosen to be buried in Taos. The place obviously meant a great deal to him despite the friction, the dissonance that followed him everywhere he went in New Mexico.

Fernando wondered. Maybe that's why Hopper and now his ghost had returned—to finally make peace with a place he loved but unintentionally offended while he lived here.

14

Later, after checking on Lacy, Antonio rode with Fernando in the Cherokee back to Taos Plaza and up to Michael's Kitchen for a quick lunch. An old hippie hangout, Michael's had become a landmark in Taos, almost as iconic as the Sagebrush Inn. Fernando parked the Cherokee in the lot alongside the storefront and the two of them walked around to the front entrance. The minute they stepped through the door Stella, one of the waitresses he knew from previous visits, spotted him and yelled across the room, "Well, I'll be, Fernando Lopez!"

Stella came bouncing over to their table with a big smile on her face, a tiny woman with long gray hair who always dressed in masculine clothes. Today she wore her usual jeans with a pearl-button western shirt. "Why, I haven't seen you since you and old Hank Mathews used to come in together back when he was still sheriff. Where you been hidin', Fernando?"

Fernando laughed. "After I retired from the Santa Fe Police, I worked as a private investigator for a while, now I call myself a fixer. I don't get up to Taos as much as I used to."

"No kidding," Stella said, smiling. "But what's a fixer? Can you fix my dishwasher, it's been broke almost a week now?"

Fernando laughed. "No, I help people get out of the messes they make for themselves," Fernando said. "I fix their problems."

"Hah! I bet that keeps you busy. Lord knows I got some messes to clean up," Stella replied. "Most of them with my ex-husband Larry, who up and married a woman half his age and now needs money. From the house I'm living in!"

"Hey, my service is *pro bono* for you, Stella," Fernando said, joking.

Stella's eyes lit up. "Now I might even be able to afford *pro bono*!"

"What do you hear from Hank these days?" Fernando asked,

eager to change the subject. He'd worked with Hank on several cases, including Taos Vendetta, Taos Gothic, and the Painted Skull Ranch case.

"As far as I know he's still living with his son in Tucson, taking it easy," Stella said.

Fernando smiled. "Yep, that's the last I heard too."

"So what can I get you boys?" Stella asked, getting down to business.

Fernando and Antonio both ordered Green Chile cheeseburgers with fries and Modelo drafts. Fernando picked at his food, having lost his appetite at the cemetery. On the other hand, Antonio devoured his entire plate quickly, as if he hadn't eaten in days. The big man took his time finishing his Modelo, though. He leaned back in his chair and sighed.

"So after we deliver Lacy to Luz I think I'll head back to Santa Fe, if that's okay with you," Fernando said.

Antonio seemed surprised but said, "Okay, whatever you need to do. I don't want to hold you up if you need to get back."

"What exactly is this crossover ceremony anyway?" Fernando asked. "Does she actually help him cross over, or just prepare him for it when the moment comes. I'm not sure I understand."

Antonio shook his head. "Good question. I don't know. When we drop Jack off, will that be the last time we see him alive? I wish I knew. I'd like a chance to say goodbye properly."

"Properly? I wonder about that. How do you say goodbye properly?" Fernando asked.

Antonio stared at Fernando for several long seconds and then said, "Hell...I don't know, Fernando. I'm just trying to get through this. I don't know what I'm supposed to do. Just trying to help an old buddy however I can."

That brought an abrupt end to their conversation. Antonio seemed a bit pissed, maybe because Fernando had announced he intended to leave after dropping Lacy off at Luz's house.

After Fernando paid the bill, the two of them drove in silence back to the Luhan House. When they pulled into the parking lot Antonio jumped out of the Cherokee and ran to the Gate House to check on Lacy. Fernando took his time. As before he was in no particular hurry, since they had a couple of hours to kill before taking Lacy to the crossover ceremony with Luz. He walked up toward the big house, noticing the dark blue peaks of the Taos Mountains were visible behind the big house. He wondered if the trail behind the Luhan property crossed Taos Pueblo land and extended all the way to the mountains? Sounded like a better way to spend the afternoon than their current death watch. Wouldn't it be nice?

On the way to the fence behind the Luhan House that marked the beginning of Taos Pueblo land he heard tires screeching on Morada Lane. He gritted his teeth, expecting trouble. Moments later the red Mustang came careening into the parking lot, spewing dust and gravel as it went. The two punks from California.

As soon as the Mustang came to rest, the blond kid and his companion jumped out. The big guy now wore a baby blue jersey with 'Bruins' in yellow print. They stopped when they spotted Fernando.

"Where's Frankenstein?" the blond kid shouted.

Fernando had no idea if the kid meant Lacy or Antonio.

"Frankenstein and the corpse he was dragging around," the blond kid continued. "Right out of the movies! Boris fucking Karloff!"

The big guy with the Bruins shirt laughed.

Fernando controlled his anger and decided to have a talk with the young punks, just like he'd done with his daughters on occasion, a fatherly talk to give them some good advice. Worth a try. So he meandered over to their Mustang with a smile on his face, the friendliest smile he could muster under the circumstances. "Hey guys, lighten up, will you? The elderly man is dying, and the big guy is taking care of him until he passes. A little kindness goes a long way, you know. So be respectful. Treat people the way you wanna be treated."

"Oh, piss off," the guy with the Bruins shirt replied.

Realizing he would have to take a slightly different approach, Fernando said, "Listen to me you little fucker, that big guy is an ex Marine and police sergeant, he's six-eight and two hundred and eighty pounds—he could tear you apart limb from limb. I've seen him do it. Understand?"

"The bigger they come, the harder they fall," the punk shot back and pulled out a pistol from under his shirt. He started waving what looked like a Glock 9 mm. around wildly with his finger on the trigger.

"Put the gun away—you'll just get yourself in trouble," Fernando said, a sense of urgency in his voice.

Suddenly the pistol exploded. The bullet pinged across the parking lot and struck the stone wall at the far end.

The kid wearing the Bruins shirt looked at his pistol as if he didn't know how it fired.

A moment later Antonio came flying out of the Gate House Cottage, as did Francis Rose out of the big house. Antonio wasted no time. He raced up to the punk with the gun. The kid stood frozen, his mouth wide open, just as surprised as everyone else that the pistol had fired.

Without speaking, Antonio backhanded the punk with his left hand, sending the kid flying back on his ass. Antonio quickly reached down and grabbed the Glock and then yanked it out of the kid's hand.

"Hey, that's my gun," the punk said.

Antonio kicked the kid in the side and said, "Shut up!" He took the clip out of the Glock and put it in his pocket.

"Thank you," Francis said, joining them.

Antonio handed her the pistol. "Keep this. Don't give it to them until they leave. Or just throw it away. Up to you."

"Oh, they'll be leaving right now," she said to the two punks. "You get your stuff together and leave. If you're still here in one hour I'll call the Taos Police and have them throw you out. Do you understand?"

The blond kid nodded, shrinking back from Antonio.

"What was that?" Antonio asked, moving toward the kid.

"Okay! We're leaving," the blond kid said, moving away from Antonio with a terrified look on his face. He helped his friend get to his feet and the two of them scurried across the parking lot, eager to get away from Antonio.

Fernando turned to Antonio. "Thanks for not killing the kid," he said, partly in jest.

"I thought about it," Antonio snarled. The big man was not amused.

15

As the time approached to take Lacy to Luz for the crossover ceremony Antonio became more nervous. He couldn't sit still, pacing through the Gate House Cottage and around the patio. "I wonder—are you sure taking Jack to this curandera is a good idea?" he asked Fernando finally. "I mean, what does a curandera do during the crossover ceremony? I'm worried about leaving Jack with someone I know nothing about. She could be a charlatan—or a murderer."

"You're the one who made the arrangements," Fernando said. "A curandera is just a naturopathic healer. I don't know what a crossover ceremony involves. I've never seen one."

That did not ease Antonio's fear, but when the time came he went in the bedroom to get Lacy, who was awake and eager to go. Unfortunately, Lacy could no longer walk, so Antonio picked up the old man and carried him out to the Wrangler, placing the gaunt, emaciated figure on the back seat. He buckled Lacy's seat belt and climbed into the driver's seat. "Are you coming?" he asked Fernando, who stood off to the side of the Wrangler watching.

Fernando hesitated, not sure what he should do. Take his leave when he had the chance, or go along to offer his support. "Do you want me to come along?" Fernando asked, hoping for a negative response. He was disappointed.

"Yes...if you would."

Sighing, Fernando climbed into the front passenger's seat and buckled up. "Where are we going?"

"According to what Luz said, we go east on Kit Carson Road toward Angel Fire and then turn right on Highway Five Eighty-five," Antonio replied, handing Fernando the card with the map Luz had given him. "Her house sets back from the road about a half-mile down the highway in a stand of trees. She said the driveway is right after a dry arroyo."

Pulling out of the parking lot they couldn't help but notice that the red Mustang with California license plates had already left. Blondie and UCLA had taken off. Good riddance.

Lacy sat stiffly on the back seat watching the outskirts of Taos flash by in his rear window.

When they reached Highway 585, they turned left and headed east. Antonio slowed down looking for the dry arroyo and Luz's driveway. Moments later he spotted the arroyo and turned into the driveway, a curving dirt road that led to an old frame house nestled in a growth of cottonwood trees. The Victorian-looking house had a wrap-around porch and a cupola on its roof, not all that common in Taos and northern New Mexico. Lots of Victorian looking houses in Santa Fe and Las Vegas, New Mexico, but not many up here in Taos. The notable exception was, of course, the Mabel Dodge Luhan House, half mud palace and half Victorian Gothic.

The driveway ended in a dirt parking lot, where a Honda CRV was parked next to an ancient, faded VW van with flat tires that looked like it had been abandoned years ago. Antonio parked next to the CRV and turned to Fernando. "Why don't you stay with Jack while I find out where to take him," Antonio said. "I'll be back to carry him in as soon as I find out."

Fernando nodded. He glanced at Lacy, who had nodded off again in the back seat, his chin resting on his chest. Lacy looked half dead already. Fernando began to wonder if Lacy would even live long enough to participate in his crossover ceremony. If not, the ceremony would be a total waste of time and money. Not that it mattered since Antonio was using Lacy's money, supposedly as much as five hundred grand in their joint bank account.

Antonio walked up to the door of the house and knocked. The door opened and the big man went inside, reappearing seconds later. He walked back and opened the rear door of the Wrangler. "Jack, I'm taking you in for the crossover ceremony now, okay?" Antonio said.

Lacy opened his eyes and nodded.

Antonio reached in and picked up Lacy, one arm under his legs and the other behind his back. He carried Lacy up to the house, where

Luz held the door open for them. Fernando followed them into the dark house, surrounded on three sides by pine and cottonwood trees.

Wearing her same purple clothes, with pendants and necklaces dangling from her neck, Luz escorted them down a long hallway, which divided the house. To the right Fernando saw a sitting room and kitchen, to the left a long room that served as a work space. The long hallway ended at what looked like two small bedrooms, one on either side of the hallway.

Fernando saw Luz's brother Daniel standing in the doorway to one of the bedrooms watching them. When Daniel noticed Fernando was staring at him, he ducked into the dark bedroom and disappeared from sight. The more Fernando saw of Daniel, the stranger Luz's brother seemed.

Antonio carried Lacy into the long dark room that reeked of strong incense. Heavy curtains on the windows made the room even darker. Fernando followed Antonio into the darkness. He could make out what appeared to be an examining or massage table at the front of the room, surrounded by cabinets. Further down he saw a bed next to a long table on which candles and incense burned. As he came closer to the table, covered by a heavy spread similar to an altar cloth, he found a collection of beads, crosses, amulets and a few other reliquaries he couldn't identify, alongside small ceramic bowls containing oils, powdered herbs, and what Fernando assumed were other naturopathic medicines.

Fernando watched as Antonio placed Lacy gently on the bed. Lacy was awake now, with his eyes wide open, waiting. "He's here," Lacy whispered. "I can see him now."

Luz stood beside the bed holding Lacy's hand. She squeezed his hand and nodded.

Beginning to feel awkward, Fernando wondered what he and Antonio were expected to do during the crossover ceremony. Help out in some way? Leave? He had no idea.

Luz whispered something in Lacy's ear and then came over to where Fernando and Antonio were standing back, trying to stay out of her way. "We're all set. He's ready," she said.

Antonio nodded. "What can we do? How can we help?"

"Nothing at the moment," Luz said. "You need to give us two or three hours to complete the ceremony. Why don't you come back about six o'clock. By then I should know."

That puzzled Fernando. Know what?

"So you don't need us?" Antonio asked.

Luz shook her head. "No...it's better that you leave. What he needs now is peace, so he can cross."

"Okay...good," Antonio said, looking around the room. "I guess we'll go back to the Gate House Cottage and come back about six then. Let us know if you need us earlier."

Fernando bit his tongue. He had a dozen questions he wanted to ask Luz, but this wasn't his show. He had to remind himself that he was only helping, if you could call it that.

Antonio hesitated, glancing at Lacy one last time, and then turned and walked out of the dark room.

Fernando followed Antonio outside to the Wrangler. They climbed in and headed back to the Gate House Cottage. When they pulled into the big parking lot at the Luhan House, they sat there in silence for several minutes, neither of them wanting to voice their thoughts. Finally Antonio broke the silence. "It feels weird leaving without Jack. I have a bad feeling about this. I'm all sixes and sevens. I don't know what to do...you wanna go to the Sagebrush for a beer?"

"You read my mind," Fernando responded. "And just so you know, I feel the same way about this. I hope we're doing the right thing."

Antonio fired up the Wrangler again and drove back to Pueblo del Sur heading south.

Something about their conversation with Luz began to bother Fernando. Finally he couldn't help himself but ask, "By the way, what did Luz mean when she said that by six o'clock she should know? Know what?"

"I have no idea," Antonio replied.

"If Lacy had crossed over?" Fernando asked, not expecting an answer.

None came.

16

Fernando checked the time. Just after five o'clock. About an hour to kill before Luz asked them to return. They were still at the Sagebrush Inn, sitting outside on the patio overlooking the mesa that stretched west all the way to the horizon. One beer had led to another, so they'd decided to stay for a light dinner. Now they were finished and waiting for their server to bring the check. When she did, Antonio passed the check across the patio table to Fernando, as usual.

"Hey—I thought you had a fat expense account or something, courtesy of Lacy," Fernando said.

Antonio shrugged. "Why not? This one's on Jack," he said, taking a card out of his wallet and slapping it on the table. The server snatched it and returned a few moments later with a slip for Antonio to sign.

Just then Antonio's cell phone rang. He took the phone out of his pocket and answered.

Fernando could hear the voice of Luz coming through Antonio's phone. She sounded different, not her usual strong, self-assured voice. Not exactly hysterical, but seriously worried. "Did you pick up Mister Lacy?"

"What? What do you mean?" Antonio asked. He bolted up, knocking over his chair, and began walking away from the table. The chair crashed on the floor, causing everyone on the patio to look their way.

"What do you mean?" Antonio barked.

"Mister Lacy crossed over. Did you pick him up? That's what I mean," Luz responded.

"No!" Antonio shouted. "We left him with you....what are you talking about? Why would we pick him up?"

After a long silence, the voice at the other end of the line became faint, fading in and out: "crossed over...went to Albertsons for flowers... got back...he was gone...don't know what...my brother...."

Antonio cut her off. "That's enough! We're on our way!" He slipped his cell phone in his shirt pocket and hurried over to the table.

"I don't fucking believe this—she says Jack crossed over but his body has disappeared," Antonio said to Fernando. "She went out to get flowers at Albertsons and the body was gone when she got back."

"I heard," Fernando said.

Antonio signed the credit card slip and waved at the server. Then he turned and ran out of the patio into the parking lot. Fernando followed, wary of this turn of events. A curandera, a crossover ceremony, and now a missing body, it was all too much. He smelled foul play.

Fernando berated himself. He should have taken the opportunity to leave when they dropped off Lacy. Why did he persist in this craziness?

They scrambled into the Wrangler and buckled up. "Goddamnit, I knew I shouldn't have left Jack. What could have happened to him? Is he alive? Did he come back and just walk away?"

Fernando held his tongue. He had no idea. And there was nothing he could say or do that would reassure Antonio. It was hopeless to even try.

Antonio raced down Kit Carson Road to the junction of Highway 585. When they pulled into Luz's driveway they found her sitting in a rocking chair on her wrap-around porch. Her eyes were closed tight. She didn't move, even when they slammed shut the doors of the Wrangler and walked up to the porch. She appeared to be in a trance, maybe meditating.

"Jesus Christ," Antonio said, stepping up on the porch and touching Luz's arm. "Are you dead?"

Her eyelids fluttered and then she opened them wide, looking at Antonio. "No, I'm not dead. I was trying to make contact in order to check on Mister Lacy. I'm not getting through. There seems to be a lot of interference. That's not a good sign, you know."

Frustrated, Antonio threw his hands up in the air. "Great. That's just what I wanted to hear."

Fernando intervened, afraid the conversation could devolve into an angry shouting match. "So what happened? Where is he?"

Luz began rocking back and forth ever so gently, back and forth.

She didn't speak at first. Then she sighed and said, "He crossed over about four o'clock. It was peaceful. He was talking to his friend Dennis, who met him on the other side. A very beautiful passing."

"Okay, but where's his body?" Antonio asked. "Did he come back to life and walk off somewhere?"

"I can't imagine that," Fernando interjected. "He could barely walk when we left him."

Luz shook her head. "I don't know. Like I said, I went to Albertsons to get flowers, and when I returned the body was missing—gone! It had just disappeared into thin air."

Fernando did not believe in coincidence, and he for damned sure didn't believe in otherworldly explanations. He believed in a material world of cause and effect, pure and simple. If Lacy's body had suddenly disappeared, then someone must have taken it. But who? And why? What was the point of stealing a dead body? What can you do with a dead body? It was all too grotesque.

"Before I called you, I went outside and walked around the house just to make sure Mister Lacy didn't wake up and try to walk away," Luz added. "But I didn't see him or any evidence that he'd left the house."

While Luz talked, Fernando remembered something Luz had said earlier. "You mentioned your brother when you called," he said. "Why did you mention your brother? What did you mean?"

Luz grimaced. "Nothing, really. I don't know what I was thinking or why I said that."

Fernando remembered her brother Daniel's reaction to hearing Lacy brag about his millions. Daniel seemed very interested. Too interested. Not only that, but Fernando remembered Daniel watching them as they brought Lacy into the house for the crossover ceremony, as if he'd been planning something. Something devious.

"Well, can you show us the bed again?" Antonio asked.

Luz nodded and led them inside. The long room was pitch black now, given the hour. Luz hit the light switch and the room flooded with bright light. They saw bunches of flowers on the bed where Lacy had lain. A knot of twisted blankets and sheets had fallen on the floor at the foot of the bed. Nothing in the room suggested a struggle had occurred. Not surprising, since a dead man didn't offer much resistance to being moved —or kidnapped, if kidnap was the correct word for stealing a body with the intent of demanding a ransom. The more Fernando thought about it, the more plausible kidnapping seemed. What else could explain the missing body? Body snatchers or little green aliens from UFOs? Not even in Taos, where the counterculture still thrived and people still believed in alternate realities.

"So you're saying you have no idea who might have taken the body?" Fernando tried again.

She shook her head. "No. I have no idea who would have done this...or why anyone would steal a body."

"About how long were you gone when you drove into Taos to get flowers at Albertsons?"

'Not long, less than half an hour," Luz replied. "I didn't stop to talk to anyone, not even the cashier, who's a friend of mine."

"So whoever took the body had to have acted fast. That indicates he—or they—knew the lay of the land," Fernando said, not wanting to let Luz off the hook. Not just yet. She seemed to be holding something back.

Luz did not reply.

Antonio paced around the room looking for clues, anything. "I don't care about the details. What matters is that we find him. Soon."

Fernando disagreed about the details but held his tongue.

"I mean, who steals a corpse? What can you do with a corpse?" Antonio continued. "Medical research?"

Luz stared at Antonio as if she thought he'd lost his mind.

Fernando stepped out of the room and went to the front door of the house, where he examined the lock on the door. The lock was untouched. No one had jimmied the lock to break into the house. It had to be an inside job.

He walked back and rejoined Antonio and Luz. "You should call the Taos Police," Fernando said.

Luz nodded. "I did. They told me to come in and file a report. I don't know if they took me seriously. I heard someone in the background laugh and say, "Dead man walking.""

"Except it's not very funny," Antonio said. He looked to Fernando for ideas, as he always had in their long history. "What'll we do?"

Fernando turned to Luz. "I think you should go in and file a report, as they suggested. You might also call the Taos County Sheriff, Chris Perez, because your property is outside the Taos city limits. File a report with him, if he thinks it would help. Other than that, I don't know what else we can do, other than wait and see if anyone gets in touch with you demanding a ransom for the return of the body. That's the only explanation I can think of at the moment—at least it's the only one that makes any sense."

"Ransom for a dead body?" Antonio asked.

"Exactly," Fernando said. "Why else would they steal a body?"

Luz stood in the center of the room shaking her head. "I wonder... what if he did come back? What if he crossed back over? Maybe his friend on the other side told him it wasn't his time...that he should go back."

Now Fernando shook his head. This was getting ridiculous. Dead men don't walk —and dead men don't come back from the dead. Unless, of course, Lacy hadn't died. Maybe he'd suffered a seizure, a bout of AFib, a temporary stoppage of the heart, or some sort of similar medical condition? He knew from experience that this phenomenon was possible.

Fernando walked up to Luz and touched her arm. "Are you positive Lacy was dead? Could he have awakened after a temporary seizure or heart flutter, something like that?"

"No—he was dead," Luz replied. "There was no pulse...he'd stopped breathing...even his color had started to change. He'd definitely passed. That's the one thing I'm sure about."

"Then where is he?" Antonio asked.

Luz rolled back her eyes. She seemed to be meditating, as if she had fallen into a trance-like state. When she spoke, her tone of voice had changed to a somber preacher's mode: "Let's all remember that there are centuries of stories—from religion, witches tales, and mythology—of people coming back from the Land of the Dead. Maybe Jack Lacy is walking among us now."

"Then where the hell is he?" Antonio repeated.

Fernando rolled his eyes. Welcome to the world of witches.

17

The answer to Antonio's question wasn't exactly blowing in the wind, but it did arrive the next morning via radio waves on his cell phone. Fernando and Antonio were sitting on the patio of the Gate House Cottage after breakfast when they heard a loud ping. For a moment Fernando thought it was Estelle texting him to see if he were coming home today, but then he saw Antonio grab for his phone and click on the text.

"Holy shit!" Antonio said, while reading the text.

"What is it?" Fernando asked.

Antonio handed his phone to Fernando, who read: "If you want the body of Jack Lacy back, bring a hundred thousand dollars in twenties and fifties to the Rio Grande Gorge Bridge parking lot on the west side of the bridge this afternoon at five o'clock exactly. Come alone and unarmed."

"So I was right," Fernando said. "I expected something like this. I wonder if Luz's brother is involved. I saw him focus like a laser when Lacy bragged that he had millions of dollars."

"I noticed," Antonio agreed. "What should we do?"

Fernando sighed. He thought for a long moment. "Well, if you do have access to that kind of money, which you mentioned earlier, you could get money from a bank and meet them at the Rio Grande Gorge Bridge. Problem is, there's no guarantee they'll actually bring Lacy's body to hand over."

Antonio nodded.

"Or you could forget the money and try to overpower them—if they have Lacy," Fernando said. "That's risky too, depending on how many of them show up at the bridge."

"You keep saying 'you'—aren't you going to stick around to help?" Antonio asked.

Though he regretted it even as he spoke, Fernando said, "Yeah...I suppose. But that's it. Once we get the body back, I'm finished. Understand? I'm heading back to Santa Fe."

"I understand," Antonio said, smiling.

Fernando shook his head, disgusted with himself. How many times had he threatened to head back to Santa Fe after this or that development? And yet here he was saying the same thing again, still stuck in Taos with no end in sight.

"I appreciate your help, Fernando...." Antonio was saying.

"Okay, but first, before we make any definitive plans, let's go talk to Luz about her brother," Fernando said. "Try to get a better sense of whether he's responsible—and if so, whether he's likely acting alone or in cahoots with others, a goddamn cabal of body snatchers or something equally bizarre. Who knows up here. This is fucking voodoo land."

Before leaving Fernando loaded his Smith & Wesson and strapped on the holster. Antonio declined to take a weapon, saying again that he didn't need one to deal with these amateurs. He was usually right, but Fernando didn't like taking chances, especially in situations where he didn't know who he was dealing with or what to expect. He'd been burned too often.

They climbed into Antonio's Wrangler and drove around to Highway 585. Turning into Luz's driveway they were relieved to see her Honda CRV. Antonio pulled in behind the CRV, blocking it. She wouldn't be going anywhere until she answered some questions.

As he stepped out of the Wrangler Fernando spotted Luz walking down from the foothills behind her house. In one hand she held the handle of a large basket, which she swung back and forth as she made her way slowly, carefully down a narrow path that looked like an old animal trail. Today she wore jeans and a sweater with her purple shawl draped around her shoulders. When she saw them she stopped and waved at them from the hill.

"There she is," Fernando said, pointing to the hill.

"I see her," Antonio replied. "What's she carrying in her basket?"

Fernando ignored Antonio's question. They waited at the Wrangler for several long minutes while Luz negotiated the hill. When she neared the bottom of the hill, they walked up to the wrap-around porch to wait for her.

"Don't mind if I do," Fernando said, sitting in one of the rocking chairs on the porch. The rocking chair felt pretty damn good. Maybe he should do what Estelle wanted and really retire for good.

Antonio, on the other hand, paced back and forth on the porch waiting impatiently for Luz.

"Did you find him?" Luz asked as she walked up to the porch, setting her basket on the ground. The basket contained a tangle of plants and flowers she had collected in the foothills.

Before Fernando could answer, Antonio pointed to the basket and asked, "What were you doing up there?"

"Wildcrafting—gathering medicinal herbs," Luz replied. "In particular, I'm looking for valerian, osha, and anemone." She glanced from Antonio to Fernando. "So did you find him?"

Antonio shook his head. He took out his cell phone and clicked on the kidnapper's text. "Take a look at this—and then we need to talk."

Luz took the phone and read the text. As she did a shadow came over her face. "Oh...I had no idea," she said nervously, obviously disturbed by what she'd just seen on the phone.

"Yeah...and we need you to come clean about your brother," Fernando said, bluntly. "He looked very interested when Lacy said he had millions of dollars. Too interested, if you ask me. Could he be involved in the kidnapping?"

Luz looked away. She sighed. "It's possible. Daniel is a bit 'slow,' as some people say. He's never been able to work much or hold down a job. Lately he's been hanging out with a guy by the name of Art Stokes, an older man who has a long criminal record, including breaking and entering, bribery and extortion, you name it. Since Daniel connected with Stokes he's been arrested for shoplifting and breaking and entering too. So yes, it's possible that Daniel and Stokes took the body and are trying to get money out of you."

Fernando frowned and shook his head sadly. The situation just seemed to get worse every day.

"Daniel was in the house when I left to get flowers at Albertsons," Luz continued. "It's possible that Art Stokes came over to join him. Stokes has been hanging around here a lot lately. I don't trust him one bit."

"Sounds to me like this Stokes could be our kidnapper," Antonio said.

"But please, whatever you do, don't hurt Daniel," Luz continued.

"He's like a child in some ways. It's just...he has a hard time fitting in... making his way in this world...like a lot of people who can't compete and fall off the map...."

"I don't have any intention of hurting anyone," Antonio replied. "I just want to find Jack's body and get it buried in Jesus Nazareno Cemetery so I can go back to Alamosa to help my son."

Luz studied Antonio's face. "I believe you."

Fernando stepped in to end the love fest. "Okay, so where can we find this Art Stokes?"

"Art lives on the outskirts of Arroyo Seco in an old farmhouse," Luz said. "Daniel has been going back and forth between my house and Art's, staying with me for a couple of days and then going to stay with Art for a few days. He's never had a place of his own. I've tried to convince him to stay away from Art, but Daniel won't listen to me. He likes Art because Art treats him like an equal, whereas lots of people around here don't. Daniel had a hard time making friends all through high school. He finally dropped out before graduating."

Fernando nodded, beginning to understand if not sympathize with Daniel.

After a long silence, Luz asked, "So what are you going to do?"

Fernando glanced at Antonio. What were they going to do?

Antonio shook his head. "Arroyo Seco?"

18

The last place Fernando wanted to go was Arroyo Seco. He'd had too many bad experiences there, most notably in his Taos Gothic and Painted Skull Ranch cases. The place was a hangout for old hippies left over from Taos's counterculture days and, in Fernando's mind anyway, for misfits and ne'er-do-wells. Nothing but trouble. That was his view of Arroyo Seco.

Yet here he was, riding shotgun in Antonio's Wrangler as they drove from the eastern outskirts of Taos all the way around Paseo del Pueblo Norte to the western side of Taos. Antonio turned right on Highway 150, also known as the Ski Valley Road because it continued up the mountain to the famous Taos Ski Valley. Moments later they drove into the tiny village of Arroyo Seco, a Sesame Street smorgasbord of brightly colored arts and crafts shops. Trimmed in blue, red, and yellow, the adobe and frame buildings were in various stages of disrepair. They included pottery and fine art galleries, restaurants, and a general store.

Antonio pulled up in front of Arroyo Seco Mercantile, an artsy building with a long porch in front surrounded by a bank of red and pink hollyhocks. Colorful handmade clothing and assorted weavings hung on the porch ceiling, which was painted bright turquoise. The place was a riot of color. A sign over the door read 'Under New Ownership.' The last time Fernando stopped at the Mercantile, under the old ownership, the place reeked of pot.

This time Fernando let Antonio lead the way into the mercantile, half art gallery and half hardware store. The clerk, an older man with short white hair and bright red suspenders holding up his jeans, sat on a bar stool behind the front counter reading a dog-eared paperback. He looked up and smiled broadly, revealing a couple of missing teeth. "Howdy, gents. What can I do for you?"

"Yeah...we're looking for Art Stokes," Antonio said, walking up to the counter. "Can you tell us where he lives?"

The clerk eyed Antonio suspiciously, rubbing the gray stubble on his face with his right hand. "You the law?"

Antonio laughed. "Not anymore. I'm retired. He just has something of mine I need to get back."

The clerk smiled again. "If it's money, you're not alone. Art owes money to just about everybody around these parts."

"So I hear. But no, he has something else of mine. Can you help us out?" Antonio asked.

"Sure, go back down the highway and take a left on Reach Road," the clerk replied, continuing to rub the sides of his face. "He lives off a county road about a mile up. Ain't much of a driveway—just a narrow dirt road overgrown with weeds. You'll see a bunch of old, abandoned cars in the distance as you drive in. That'd be his place. You can't miss it."

"Okay, that's easy enough," Antonio said.

"I gotta warn you, it's not much to look at—just like old Art himself," the clerk said, laughing.

"What's he driving these days?" Antonio asked.

"Well, he has a whole yard filled with junkers," the clerk said. "Last time I saw him he was driving an old Chevy van, two-tone, supposed to be green and white, 'cept both the green and white are faded to the same color of gray. Van looks like it's made outta putty."

"Thanks...much appreciated," Antonio said, turning to go.

"Good luck. What's he have of yours, anyway?" the clerk asked. "Good thing it ain't money, because you'd never see it again."

Antonio stopped and turned back. "A dead body."

Fernando watched the clerk's mouth fall open, ending the conversation once and for all. The clerk's mouth moved but nothing came out as Fernando followed Antonio out the door of the mercantile.

They climbed back in the Wrangler and drove back down Highway 150 to Reach Road. Antonio slowed down when he turned onto the unmarked county road mentioned by the clerk. The so-called driveway turned out to be a narrow brown slash in the mesa, mostly overgrown with weeds and dead tumbleweeds blown hither and thither by the winds that whipped across the mesa.

Antonio slowed to a crawl now, negotiating half-buried rocks and sometimes deep ruts. As they drew closer they saw the extent of the automobile graveyard ahead. Must have been nine or ten vehicles, some up on blocks, others with their entrails extracted and tossed haphazardly on the flat mesa.

"Jesus, what a fucking dump," Antonio said, twisting the steering wheel to the right and then the left to avoid obstacles in the road.

Eventually they approached the house, a gray tumbledown frame house that sagged in the middle. The house seemed to sink into the ground, a dirt lot with scattered weeds. Two of its windows were boarded up and covered with plastic sheets. Most of the shingles had long since fallen off the pitched roof, leaving patches of black tarpaper over exposed particle board. Behind the house stood a wooden outhouse in much the same dilapidated condition. Off to the side stood the entrance to an underground root cellar and a pump house, with an old-fashion pump on a slab of concrete, the kind that you had to pump by hand.

Further down the yard Fernando saw a small red barn with a partially collapsed roof. Off to the side of the barn a small wooden corral held two scraggly cows that appeared to be either asleep or frozen in place, as still as bronze statues. The cows stood beside a small metal water tank fed by another manual hand-pump. There wasn't an electrical wire or pole in sight. Meaning the place did not have running water or electricity.

"No sign of a Chevy van," Antonio said, parking the Wrangler near the door of the house, a rusted metal door with huge dents in the bottom of the door, as if it had been kicked repeatedly.

Fernando stayed in the Wrangler, not interested in seeing the inside of the house. The outside was enough of an eye sore, thank you. On the other hand Antonio jumped out and walked to the metal door, which opened as soon as he touched it. Antonio motioned for Fernando to join him.

Cursing to himself, Fernando followed Antonio inside the house, a dark hovel with a few pieces of beat-up furniture: a sofa, a single bed, a kitchen table, and a couple of kitchen chairs. Dirty blankets on the bed and sofa indicated where the two men had been sleeping. The kitchen counter was nothing more than a slab of particle board setting on two wooden sawhorses. No stove or refrigerator, only a large Igloo cooler for camping. Fast food containers and bags of garbage littered one entire corner of the floor, where they heard rodents scurrying around on the wooden slat floors. Depressing didn't even begin to describe the place.

"I gotta get out of here—the place stinks!" Antonio said.

Fernando didn't need any persuasion. He ducked out the door first, before Antonio.

"Let's check out the root cellar," Fernando said, pointing to the door to the underground chamber. "That would be a perfect place to hide a body—embalmed or not embalmed."

"Yeah, maybe they canned Lacy," Antonio joked.

Fernando laughed. "Canned?"

They walked around to the underground cellar and found the door unlocked, with an open padlock dangling from the latch. When they opened the door a burst of rank moldy air accosted them. The steps down were dug out of the earth with broken pieces of flagstone laid on top of the earthen steps. Fernando took out his cell phone and clicked on the flashlight app. He led the way down into the dark cellar, entering a narrow room with shelves on both sides stacked with jars of canned vegetables that looked ancient, if not prehistoric! He found a smaller empty room off to the side, perfect for storing a corpse. But the only corpse they found turned out to be a large dead rat, half devoured by other unknown predators.

"Shit!" Antonio cursed, pulling a handkerchief out of his rear pocket and holding it tightly over his nose and mouth. "Everything smells rotten down here, even without a corpse."

Fernando was about to do the same when he heard a noise coming from the door at the top of the root cellar, followed by a loud click. Had Art Stokes returned? He hurried up the steps, aided by the flashlight, and tried to open the door. Locked! Someone had replaced the padlock on the latch and snapped it closed. They were locked in the root cellar.

"What's wrong?" Antonio asked from below.

"Someone locked the padlock on the door."

"Are you serious?" Antonio asked, making his way slowly up the stairs. He tried the door and likewise found it locked.

Cursing, Antonio said, "Stand back. Give me some room. He put the handkerchief back in his pants.

Fernando shuffled down the stairs to the bottom floor and waited.

Antonio steadied himself on the third or fourth step down and raised his massive right leg. Then, viciously, he kicked the door using all of his two hundred and eighty pounds for leverage. The wooden door burst into fragments as if blown apart by explosives. The air, now filled with dust and sawdust, made Antonio sneeze again and again. He took the handkerchief out of his pocket and smothered his nose, blowing hard into the handkerchief.

Gagging, Fernando followed Antonio through the dust into the sunshine and clean air. He waited for Antonio to stop sneezing.

When he finished blowing his nose, Antonio turned to Fernando. "Now I'm really pissed. I'll kill the motherfuckers!"

19

Fernando and Antonio sat in the Wrangler staring at the now empty Gate House Cottage. They'd had no luck finding Art Stokes after freeing themselves from his root cellar. Driving around Arroyo Seco looking for Stokes soon became an exercise in futility, so they'd returned to the Luhan House in defeat. "What do you want to do now?" Fernando asked, having reached the point of no return. Face it, he would never get back to Santa Fe. Never.

Antonio shook his head. "Hell if I know."

"We're supposed to meet them at five o'clock," Fernando reminded Antonio. "You said you have access to five hundred thousand dollars of Lacy's money in a bank account, so you could give them the hundred grand they're asking for. Face it, one hundred grand is not a lot of money these days. Or you could offer them less. My guess is they would settle for any amount you offer—both of them are impoverished and desperate. What do you think?"

Antonio did not respond.

"Even if you did give them the whole hundred grand, you would still have four hundred grand left to pay for Lacy's plot at Jesus Nazareno and the other burial expenses," Fernando added.

Antonio nodded. "I suppose I could. After I pay for the plot at Jesus Nazareno and the other expenses, I'll still have around three hundred thousand left over. It's just the idea that bothers me. Why let this pathetical little prick get away with extortion? You know what I mean?"

"I suppose," Fernando said, "but it's not your money, so why do you care? At any rate, you don't have much time to come to a decision. We're supposed to meet them this afternoon at the Rio Grande Gorge Bridge, remember?"

"Yeah, well...I don't know. Maybe we should go to the bank and get the money. Not the hundred grand, but a few thousand. Maybe you're right—maybe they would accept whatever I give them."

Fernando nodded. "Typically, banks won't let you withdraw more than twenty thousand in cash at a time," he continued. "That means you could offer Daniel and Stokes ten grand each. Maybe they would settle for that. If not, you could give them checks for the rest of what they want. Say another ten or twenty grand each. Or less. Whatever they'll settle for."

Antonio thought about that for a moment. "Yeah...I suppose...or we could just take Jack's body by force when we meet them," Antonio replied, a big smile on his face. "And if they try to stop us, I could teach them a lesson. Believe me, it would be my pleasure to break a few bones."

Fernando laughed. "I'm sure you would enjoy breaking a few bones. But here's the thing, they might not even have the body with them when they arrive at the Rio Grande Gorge Bridge."

"Then I'll wait until I see the body—what's the problem?"

Fernando sighed, throwing his hands up in the air. He was losing patience with Antonio.

"What?" Antonio asked, seeing Fernando's frustration.

Fernando did not respond. What was the point? Antonio was a hothead, thinking he could solve every problem and every threat with his physical prowess. Sometimes he could, but there had been times when his cavalier attitude had caused needless injuries, the most recent example being their shootout with the Sinaloa Cartel in the Devil on Canyon Road and Santa Fe Assassin cases. Sometimes you had to use your brains, not your brawn.

They sat uncomfortably in the Wrangler for another few minutes, neither of them speaking. Finally Antonio broke the silence. "Oh, the hell with it, let's go to the bank and get the money," Antonio said. "Maybe you're right."

Begrudgingly, Antonio hit the ignition and negotiated a U-turn in the parking lot. Once on Paseo del Pueblo Sur he drove down to the nearest branch of the US Bank. "I'll be right back," Antonio said, climbing out of the Wrangler and slamming the door closed. Wishful thinking, as it turned out.

Forty minutes later Fernando couldn't tolerate any more waiting.

He jumped out of the Wrangler and walked down the street looking for interesting shops, anything to pass the time. He found nothing of interest, so he walked back to the Wrangler and crawled into the rear seat, intending to take a nap. What the hell? Nothing else to do. But as soon as he lay back on the seat and put his feet up on the door handle, the driver's door opened and Antonio popped his big head into the cabin. "What's up with you? Did you pass out or something?" Antonio asked.

"No, I didn't pass out. What took you so long?"

"I had to sign all these goddamn papers and they still didn't want to give me the money," Antonio said. "I had to threaten to close the account and take the money across the street to a credit union before they'd hand over twenty grand. You'd think I was asking for twenty million."

"Good. So you got the money," Fernando said.

"Ten thousand dollars apiece, not a penny more. They give me any trouble, I'll kick their asses one at a time or both at the same time, it doesn't matter to me," Antonio said.

"Yeah, well I've had it," Fernando replied. "We still have several hours to kill before we're supposed to meet them. Let's go back to the Gate House Cottage and have a Modelo."

Antonio smiled. He didn't need much persuasion. "Good thing I laid in a good supply," he said.

They drove back to the Luhan House and parked in their usual spot. Antonio led the way. He walked up to the Gate House Cottage and opened the front door. Stepping inside, he froze. "What's that?" he asked.

Fernando could hear voices. Sounded like they were coming from the bedroom where Lacy had slept.

"Is that Jack's voice?" Antonio asked. "What the fuck? Did he come back to life?"

Fernando held back and let Antonio walk to the bedroom by himself. Let the big man handle it, whatever 'it' was.

"Wait!" Antonio yelled, rushing into the bedroom.

Fernando caught a glimpse, just a passing shadow, of someone or something exiting the door to the patio. "What was that?" he asked.

"He came back. Jack came back," Antonio said, standing in the doorway looking out at the empty patio. "But why? Why would he come back here, to the Gate House Cottage of all places?"

Fernando ignored the questions. Instead, he went directly to the kitchen and grabbed two cold bottles of Modelo from the refrigerator. He carried them outside to the patio where Antonio was sitting at the table now. Fernando took a Swiss Army Knife out of his pocket and opened the bottles. Then he passed one of the bottles to Antonio, who smiled and said, "Don't mind if I do."

"Maybe it was our imagination," Fernando said. "Been a long day."

Antonio drank half of his Modelo and set the bottle down. "That wasn't my imagination. Jack was here, talking to someone. Must have been Dennis Hopper. Maybe Dennis is helping him adjust. I imagine it takes some time to adjust to the land of the dead."

"I thought you didn't believe in ghosts," Fernando said.

Antonio shook his head sadly. "I don't know what to think. You do believe in ghosts, right?"

"Like I said—I don't disbelieve," Fernando replied. "All I know is that I saw something, not only here but in Ghost Ranch, Chaco Canyon, Painted Skull Ranch, and other places I don't care to revisit."

Antonio looked around the patio as if making sure no ghosts were present. "So what'll we do? How do we find out if they do really exist?" he asked.

Fernando raised his bottle of Modelo. "We drink our Modelo. What else can we do but live our lives? And anyway, what practical difference does it make if ghosts do or do not exist?"

"None...I guess," Antonio said, not sounding very convinced.

Antonio quickly finished his beer and went to get two more. Halfway through the second round, Fernando asked, "So what's going to happen to all Lacy's millions? Is he really that wealthy?"

"I think so," Antonio said. "Or he was, I should say. He gave away most of his money to veteran's organizations, especially the Wounded Warrior Project. He said about the only money left was the five hundred grand he put in our joint account at US Bank for his burial expenses."

"What will you do with what's left over after you finally get him in the ground?" Fernando asked.

Antonio shook his head. "Depends on what's left after I pay for everything—the cemetery, the funeral home, the burial, the hand-carved cross, the crossover ceremony, and then the ransom, whatever I have to pay these two bozos. Anything left I'll invest in my son's ranch. He could use the money. When he took over the place was rundown from years of neglect. We're slowly making improvements."

Fernando checked his watch.

"Yeah, I'm going crazy waiting around," Antonio said. He pulled out his leather bag of peyote and plopped it on the table. "I'm gonna need something for anxiety. Something's gotta break here soon, because I'm having a relapse. I'm on the verge of having another attack of Post Traumatic Stress Disorder."

Not what Fernando wanted to hear, even though he felt the same anxiety. "Well, just take it easy. Try to relax."

"Here, you want a button?" Antonio asked, offering the bag of peyote to Fernando.

"No thanks, I need to stay focused," Fernando said, trying to think of a distraction to take Antonio's mind off their present situation and get him to relax. "I know. It's too late for lunch and too early for dinner, but how about brunch?"

20

Fernando hadn't been to the Rio Grande Gorge Bridge since he and Antonio were chasing Jimmy Mackey all over Taos County in the Dead Go Fast case. The place had bad juju. The bridge spanned the wide Rio Grande Gorge 650 feet above the river, famous here for kayaking and other white water activities. The bridge itself was famous for one thing and one thing only: suicide. Every year several people committed suicide by jumping off the bridge and falling on the rocks below. Signs posted on the bridge directed lost souls to a suicide prevention hotline—a well-meaning, if futile attempt to stop the carnage. To Fernando's knowledge no one ever survived a jump off the Rio Grande Gorge Bridge.

They arrived early to meet the body snatchers, driving around Highway 64 to the northwest corner of Taos where the Rio Grande had cut a deep jagged channel out of the flat mesa. The gorge took your breath away when you first approached the bridge and saw the open mesa fall away and plunge two hundred yards to the river. The bridge afforded a spectacular view of the winding river below and of the mountain ranges that surrounded the mesa. It was a place of beauty and death inhabited by more ghosts than anyone could count.

A Taos paranormal once told Fernando the ghostly chatter here was so loud it created a hum when you tried to record the voices, none of which were discernible in the cacophony of sorrow. It was impossible to record only a single voice. The ghosts were legion.

Fresh from a mid-afternoon meal at Michael's Kitchen that brightened his mood and lessened his anxiety, Antonio drove across the bridge and parked in the dirt lot that served as a visitor parking lot. They sat in the Wrangler waiting, without a plan. They'd been unable to agree on a plan of action, how to deal with Daniel and Art Stokes. Finally Antonio had said, "Fuck it, we'll play it by ear."

Once again Fernando did not approve of Antonio's cavalier attitude. He preferred to have a detailed plan and to stick with it, come what may. Sure, most plans tended to come unglued once the action started, but it was better to have an agreed upon plan of action to fall back on. But this was Antonio's play, not Fernando's. He was only here to help, he had to remind himself. The one thing he'd insisted on was carrying his weapon, just in case. So he'd strapped on his Smith & Wesson before leaving the Gate House Cottage. Antonio brought his weapon but resisted wearing it. Instead, he kept it locked in the glove compartment of the Wrangler. "Not a good idea," Fernando told Antonio. "What if you need it quickly?" Antonio just shrugged.

A few minutes after five o'clock they saw the two-tone Chevy van coughing across the bridge. The van's engine sounded in desperate need of a tune-up, if not an overhaul. When the van turned into the parking lot, Antonio climbed out of the Wrangler to meet them face to face. The big man folded his arms across his massive chest and stared at the van, with not a hint of fear or even unease. He might get anxious beforehand, but once the action started, Antonio never got rattled. With his feet planted squarely on the ground, he stood staring at the van, daring the two body snatchers to come out in the open. When the situation became physical, he was in the realm where he reigned supreme.

Fernando watched as Antonio zeroed in on his prey. Neither Daniel or Art Stokes had any idea of what they were dealing with.

Stokes, all one hundred pounds of him, bounded out of the van like a little rooster, ready to brawl. In contrast, Daniel stayed put in the driver's seat and stayed behind, downright bashful. He let the van idle.

"Gotcha...you're here now...show me the money," Stokes ordered. The emaciated little man did a couple of jump steps and waved his arms. He looked like he was about to start skipping around the damn parking lot.

Fernando smiled. Without the pistol on his hip, Stokes would look like a comic book character, a laughing stock.

"Fuck you, old man!" Antonio spit out, not one to bother with diplomacy. "Where's the body?"

Stokes swatted the side of his van. "Right here. In the back. Now give me the money...then we'll give you the body."

"No! Show me the body first," Antonio said, puffing up his chest to show his bulk and walking ominously toward Stokes. He towered over the animated little man, a foot taller and at least a hundred and eighty pounds heavier. Hands twitching, he looked as though he were about to grab Stokes and rip the old man's head off. No one there doubted he could do it.

"Here...take a look," Stokes said, opening the rear compartment of the van. He danced around the open door and motioned inside, where what looked like a body was wrapped in a bedspread. Then he bent over and pulled down the top of the bedspread, revealing the withered gray face of Jack Lacy with his eyes and mouth wide open, a ghoulish sight.

Antonio turned away, finding it hard to look at Lacy's face.

Stokes cackled, sounding as though he thought this was funny for some unknown reason. "So you've seen him. Now give me the money."

Antonio stopped a few feet from Stokes with a scowl on his face. "Why didn't you close his eyes and mouth? It's disrespectful. Don't you know anything about how to care for the dead?"

"What difference does it make, dead is dead," Stokes replied. The little rooster was not backing down from Antonio.

"Get out of my way!" Antonio ordered and swatted Stokes away from the rear of the van. He bent over and took a closer look at Lacy's face. Cursing, Antonio turned and faced Stokes.

At this point Fernando decided to intervene, worried that Antonio would kill the old man. "Okay, it's time. Give him the money, Antonio," Fernando said, moving closer in case he had to intervene.

From his back pockets Antonio produced two overstuffed envelopes held together by rubber bands and handed them to Stokes one at a time. "There's ten thousand dollars in both envelopes, one for each of you," he said.

"What...wait...how much?" Stokes sputtered, his mood changing instantly from jovial to somber. He balled his fists as though he intended to fight Antonio, which would be a big mistake.

"Ten thousand for each of you," Antonio repeated. "Now stand back away from me."

"No...I said one hundred thousand dollars...that's fifty thousand each...not ten thousand measly dollars," Stokes said, sounding downright distraught, on the verge of hysteria.

Antonio shook his head. "You're too late, his money's all gone. This is all that's left. Twenty thousand dollars. Take it or leave it."

"Hah! Liar!" Stokes shouted. He pulled out his pistol, which looked like another Glock and waved it wildly at Antonio, while still clutching the two envelopes with his left hand.

A Glock! Every sonofabitch in New Mexico these days had a Glock! That was the only thing that came across Fernando's mind as he stared at what had become a standoff. Antonio was too far away to make a run at Stokes, though Fernando could tell he was itching to get his hands on the old man.

"Back off! Get back!" Stokes shouted, still waving his pistol at Antonio. Then he turned suddenly and jumped in the rear compartment next to the body, screaming to Daniel: "Go! Go!"

Daniel hit the accelerator and the van skidded off in a burst of dirt and exhaust, with Stokes and the dead body hanging out the rear. Antonio and Fernando covered their eyes. When the dust cloud cleared, they saw the van screeching to a halt midway across the bridge.

"What the hell are they doing?" Antonio asked, running a few steps toward the bridge.

While Fernando and Antonio watched from a distance, Daniel jumped out of the driver's seat and ran around back to the open rear compartment of the van. He reached in and dragged out the body of Jack Lacy, bedspread and all. Then he lugged the body over to the bridge railing and, struggling to get it on top of the railing, pushed it off the bridge with one violent lunge.

"Holy shit! Did you see that!" Antonio said.

"I saw it," Fernando replied, getting angrier by the minute. Maybe he should have let Antonio kill the old man.

They watched Lacy's body fall as if in slow motion. As it fell the bedspread unfolded and came loose flapping in the wind. Then the body spun its way down to the river. They were too far away to tell if the body fell into the water or on the rocks along the bank.

Meanwhile, Daniel climbed back in the van and took off fast, racing to the end of the bridge and disappearing over a rise.

Without saying a word to each other, Antonio and Fernando hurried back to the Wrangler, climbed on board, and roared onto the bridge. Antonio slammed on his brakes when they came to the point, halfway across the bridge, where Daniel had dropped Lacy's body over the railing.

Antonio jumped out of the Wrangler first. He grabbed his binoculars and brought them over to the railing, scouring the river and the rocky banks on either side of the fast-moving current. "Shit—I don't see the body," he said, handing the binoculars to Fernando.

Fernando looked downstream, thinking the current may have carried the body further down the Gorge toward Pilar. But he saw nothing in the water or closer up on the banks. "Nothing," Fernando said. "The current's too strong. He's probably already down the river a ways."

Antonio threw up his hands in disgust.

Once again Jack Lacy's body had disappeared.

21

The Search and Rescue team arrived shortly after six p.m. Antonio and Fernando had called Taos County Sheriff Chris Perez, who they knew from previous cases, and reported the missing body, careful to craft a believable story. They claimed Lacy, dying of Glioblastoma, wanted one last view of the beautiful Rio Grande Gorge, so they'd taken him out to the bridge where he accidently fell off trying to get a better view. A preposterous story, but the sheriff's office had dutifully taken down the information and sent out a search and rescue team, following protocol.

"About time," Antonio said, checking his watch, the only person Fernando knew who was as impatient as he was.

They watched from a viewing area near the middle of the bridge as the team steered down the river. He noticed the heavy gauge wire fence attached to the railing intended to prevent jumpers. The fence made it difficult but not impossible to jump. Sections of the fence had been cut away by wire cutters or pushed out from the railing, leaving gaps large enough for a normal sized person to squeeze through. Every few yards there was a phone connected to a suicide prevention hotline. Everything possible had been done to prevent accidents and suicides, which occurred every year despite the precautions.

The team consisted of two orange and black rafts that came bouncing down the river, careening from one rapid to the next. He counted two men on each raft, all wearing helmets and life jackets. They maneuvered among the rocks by using long poles and ropes to stay connected. As they approached the bridge they slowed to a near stop to begin their search.

The lead raft steered over against the riverbank. The men on board looped a rope around a large boulder on the bank to stabilize the raft.

Then they tossed another rope to the men on the second raft, who let the rope out slowly as they moved downstream searching the river for any sign of Lacy's body. They proceeded down the river in steps, using this same technique: one raft secured to the bank, the other raft moving slowly downstream while the men on board dredged the water with poles and hooks and their hands.

When the rafts disappeared around a bend Fernando followed Antonio farther down the bridge to get a better view. About a hundred yards down the river the search raft spotted something ahead, a black object partially submerged in the river. One of the men tried to pull the object out of the water, while the other held the rope steady. Making their work more difficult, the raft bucked and bounced in the current. The two men working together finally got hold of the object and slowly pulled it out of the churning water. Fernando could see their disappointment when it turned out to be a black garbage bag leaking garbage as they hoisted it out of the water and tossed it on the raft. This scene repeated, one false alarm after another, as they made their way slowly down the river fighting the current.

Antonio checked his watch. "They're not going to find him tonight. And by tomorrow morning the body could be halfway to Española. We might never get Jack back."

Fernando shrugged. "What can we do?"

By eight p.m. the team had searched less than a mile of the river and was fast running out of time. Soon it would be dark and impossible to see on the river. The rafts would need to head for the nearest launch site and pull out of the river. They had no choice but to wait for first light before resuming the search. Operating in the dark would be impossible— and dangerous.

While they watched the rafts pull over, Antonio's cell phone rang. "Yeah, I expected as much. Okay," he said and clicked off.

"Fuck!" Antonio said. "They'll have to pick up tomorrow morning where they're leaving off today. By that time who knows where the body might be? The current could carry it down below Pilar."

Fernando frowned. He was just as pissed. At this rate it could take days before they found Lacy's body, if ever. He needed to get back to Santa Fe. So why was he delaying?

"What do you think? Should we hike down to the river and see if we can find him?" Antonio asked, sounding desperate.

"No, it's dark, you can't see a damn thing!" Fernando fired back. "Plus, he's a long way down the river by now. As you say."

Cursing, Antonio turned and headed back to the Wrangler. Fernando followed, eager to get back to civilization, Taos or better yet Santa Fe. They climbed into the Wrangler, Antonio slamming his door closed in disgust. The big man was not a happy camper. Just then a Toyota Prius drove up behind the Wrangler and honked. Antonio glanced in the rear view mirror, not in the mood to be harassed. Sighing, Antonio climbed out of the car and walked up to the Prius, where a young man with long hair and tattoos kept motioning for him to move his Wrangler.

"Move your Jeep—there's no parking on the bridge," the young man yelled at Antonio. Big mistake.

"We're with Search and Rescue," Antonio said, towering over the Prius. "Man's fallen off the bridge here. I'd recommend you shut the fuck up and drive on by if you don't want to join him." With that Antonio opened the door of the Prius and reached into the cab of the car, grabbing the young man by the neck and lifting him up off his seat. The young man gurgled something and then tried to pry Antonio's hand off his neck, in vain.

"You understand what I'm saying?" Antonio asked.

The young man nodded and continued gurgling.

Antonio released the young man, who coughed for a few moments and then without speaking quickly backed up and drove off, eager to get away from Antonio. The big man stood there with his arms crossed across his chest watching the Prius drive away. Finally Antonio walked back to the Wrangler and climbed into the driver's seat cursing to himself.

"The kid didn't mean any harm," Fernando said.

Antonio gave Fernando the Evil Eye.

They drove in silence back to Taos. When Antonio passed by Kit Carson Road, the turnoff to the Luhan House, Fernando smiled. He knew precisely where Antonio was heading.

Turning into the parking lot of the Sagebrush Inn, Antonio parked next to the adobe wall surrounding the restaurant's outdoor patio. No matter what the situation, the big man could always eat and drink.

They walked in and helped themselves to a corner table overlooking the sprawl of the Sagebrush Inn, a scattering of adobe buildings and courtyards crisscrossed by wooden stairways and strings of white lights hanging from the trees and wooden scaffoldings. Just beyond the tumbledown buildings an open mesa stretched all the way to the mountains on the western horizon.

Antonio eased back in his patio chair and sighed. He seemed to have calmed down. "Well, I'll have to admit I'm pretty damned discouraged—I need to get back to Alamosa to help my son with the ranch."

"Tell me about it," Fernando replied. "I need to get back to Santa Fe before Estelle files for divorce."

While they talked, their sever came over to their table. An older woman with short gray hair and a name tag that read 'Janet,' she handed them menus and then looked at them sympathetically. "You two look like someone just shot your dawg," she said, clicking her tongue.

Antonio smiled, in spite of himself. "Worse. An old friend just died and we lost his body."

"Whaaaaat?" she said, shaking her head in disbelief. "How in the wild world of sports did you lose his body?"

"He's exaggerating," Fernando jumped in. "Actually the body was stolen by a couple of body snatchers who then threw it off the Rio Grande Gorge Bridge into the Rio Grande."

Janet stared at them as if they were a couple of lunatics and then walked away, still shaking her head. Inside they saw her talking to the bartender, no doubt telling him about her two crazy customers. She pointed outside to their table and said something that made the bartender laugh.

"Well, I'm glad to see we can provide some amusement," Fernando said. "At least we accomplished something today."

When she returned, they ordered their usual: combination plate for Antonio, Chicken Enchiladas with red chile for Fernando, accompanied by two ice cold Modelo drafts.

By the time their meals arrived the patio was starting to fill up with customers, the usual lively crowd at the Sagebrush, artists and leftover hippies from the good old days of Fernando's youth. Reminded him of the Canyon Road crowd in Santa Fe, what was left of it after the street, like the city, had gone corporate. Tonight some of the crowd had come for dinner and then music in the cantina, which started about eight o'clock. According to the billboard in the hall, the music would be provided by the 'Haymaker Duo—half country, half folk, and all funk.'

All of which was perfect for Fernando and Antonio, both of whom could use some entertainment, anything that would take their minds off Lacy's missing body. Loud music sounded perfect.

As it turned out, the husband and wife duo started singing just as they finished their meal. They paid the check, or rather Fernando paid the check and Antonio left a few dollars for tip, and headed inside and through the restaurant to the bar, a classic 100-year-old cantina with a hand-carved bar and huge logs holding up the equally huge vigas on the ceiling. The place seemed like an anachronism, as though it had come back in time from the Wild West.

The husband and wife duo stood at the front of the cantina behind a snarl of amps and microphones. The husband played an electric guitar, while the wife kept up on a screaming fiddle that gave their music some extra heft. Not only were they dressed alike in jeans and black western shirts, they looked identical with long stringy gray hair and deep, deep wrinkles lining their sunburned faces. No spring chickens, they'd long since passed the big five-zero.

Inside the cantina Fernando took the lead, trying to get as far away from the Haymakers as possible. He found a table for two against the rear wall and claimed it for the two of them. Antonio stopped at the bar to buy two more Modelo drafts, which he carried to the table without spilling a drop. "Why are you sitting so far away?" the big man asked.

"Just listen," Fernando said.

Just then the Haymakers began wailing an old hippie anthem, "One Toke over the Line." Except for their choice of songs, the music wasn't half bad, just loud. Loud enough to make them forget the day's events.

Sometime later Fernando hailed down the server, a young woman with red hair and nose-ring who came right over, super attentive. "Another round of Modelo, and keep them coming."

The young woman laughed. "Good call. They get better the more you drink."

"We're waiting for the folk," Fernando quipped.

Smiling, she said, "That was the folk."

22

The ringing of a cell phone woke Fernando. Thinking it was his phone, he groped for the table next to the sofa where he slept. Something fell and shattered on the floor. He opened his eyes wide and instantly remembered where he was: the Gate House Cottage at the Mabel Dodge Luhan estate. The last twenty-four hours came rushing back in his mind like a fast-forward slide show that ended last night at the Sagebrush Cantina where he and Antonio had enjoyed their share of drinks. And yet, oddly enough, he felt exhilarated this morning, better than he'd felt in days, maybe weeks. Something about the loud music and frenzied activity last night. He felt alive and full of energy this morning, still jazzed from a night of partying at the Sagebrush Inn to the funky tunes of the Haymaker Duo.

Fernando heard Antonio talking from the small bedroom in the rear of the cottage where he'd been sleeping. He seemed to be asking for directions to drive somewhere. What now? Another wild goose chase? Moments later the big man came shuffling into the living area wearing only his underwear and holding his cell phone with one hand and his head with the other. "Jesus, how much did we drink last night, do you remember?" Antonio asked.

"Who was counting?" Fernando replied, jumping up from the sofa, feeling full of energy.

Antonio shook his head. "What? Are you still high from last night? You drank almost as much as I did."

"I feel great," Fernando said. "Who was that on the phone?"

"Oh...yeah...it was search and rescue," Antonio replied, still groggy. "Two fisherman found a body early this morning at the Orilla Verde Recreation Area down river. They want me to come identify it— see if it's Jack." He looked around the room. "What time is it, anyway?"

Fernando checked his watch. "Nine o'clock. We slept late. Where is this Orilla Verde Recreation Area?"

"It's on Highway Sixty-Eight, a few miles down-river from the bridge," Antonio said. "They found the body on some rocks in the river. They want me to come down and look at the body. Immediately."

Fernando nodded, feeling too good to complain. On a day like this, anything was possible, including finishing this case and getting the hell out of Taos. The thought of leaving energized him.

"Thing is, I need coffee before I can do anything this morning," Antonio said. "Seriously."

"Then I'll go get some coffee from the breakfast buffet here," Fernando said. "We can pick up a burrito or a sausage-egg biscuit from some fast food joint along the highway."

"Okay...good plan," Antonio said, heading back to the small bedroom to get dressed.

Fernando pulled on his jeans and hiking boots and then walked over to the Luhan House for coffee. By the time he returned to the Gate House Cottage, Antonio was sitting on the sofa, dressed and ready to roll.

They drank their coffee quickly and then walked out to the parking lot. "You want me to drive this time?" Fernando asked.

"Sure, why not? I'm not even awake yet."

Fernando unlocked the Cherokee and they climbed on board. He drove out to Paseo del Pueblo Sur and stopped at the first fast food drive-thru. They gobbled their sausage-egg biscuits while driving and managed to finish by the time they passed by the San Francisco de Asis Church and drove out of Ranchos de Taos onto Highway 68 heading south.

"Breakfast of champions," Fernando said sarcastically and tossed his paper wrapper in the back seat.

Antonio mumbled something about dog food that sounded like an insult rather than a joke.

Nearing the Orilla Verde Recreation Area they spotted two Taos County Sheriff's cruisers and a Forensic van in the parking lot. Fernando pulled in on the opposite side of the parking lot to give the sheriff's vehicles more room to maneuver. They walked down to the Rio Grande, which was higher than usual at this time of year. Three uniformed officers stood next to a body laid out flat on a plastic sheet. A fourth officer, squatting on the sheet, stood up with a metal suitcase and headed back to the Forensics van as Fernando and Antonio approached.

"Damn! You can smell it—death!' Antonio said.

Fernando fought the urge to turn his head away. Not a pretty sight. Lacy's body was bloated from the gasses caused by decomposing bacteria. The Rio Grande current had pushed his shirt up to his shoulders, revealing red and yellow patches of discolored flesh on the otherwise pale, swollen abdomen. Without socks and shoes, his feet looked black. Worst of all, Lacy's face was unrecognizably swollen and distorted, a face from a torture chamber or a freak show. In death Lacy bore no resemblance to the larger-than-life professional assassin Fernando had known in Santa Fe, before his illness crippled him.

"Howdy, I'm Antonio Blake. I talked to you on the phone earlier this morning," Antonio said, walking up to the oldest of the three deputies, whose nametag read Rodgers.

Rodgers shook Antonio's hand, a barrel-chested middle-aged man with a crew cut who looked like a former athlete. "As I said on the phone, a couple of fly fishermen found him about seven o'clock on the rocks over there." He pointed to the far side of the Rio Grande. "We got the search and rescue bulletin last night and saw you were the contact person."

Antonio nodded. "Yep, that's Jack Lacy, my friend. Hell of a thing," he said, staring down at Lacy's body.

"Yessir, water can pretty near take away a man's identity—and his humanity," Rodgers said. "Forensics wants to take the body into the lab to determine cause of death. I know you said the deceased had a terminal case of Glioblastoma and likely drowned when he fell off the bridge, but they still have to verify the cause of death. After they make a determination, they'll provide a death certificate. Then you can have your mortuary pick up the body."

"Good. I've already contacted Rivera Family Funerals," Antonio said, still staring at Lacy's body.

Rodgers frowned. "I wouldn't advise an open coffin at the showing," he said solemnly.

"No showing," Antonio agreed. "He doesn't have any friends or family in Taos. He was a friend of Dennis Hopper and wanted to be buried in Jesus Nazareno Cemetery near Hopper."

Rodgers shook his head. "Jesus Nazareno's a local cemetery for people who live in Taos."

"Yeah, I know. He's paying a whole lot of money to buy a plot there. A lot of money."

"Whatever you say," Rodgers said. "Anyway, I'll have Forensics call you as soon as the death certificate is ready. Maybe later today."

"Thanks," Antonio said.

"By the way, where are you staying in town, in case I need you to sign something?"

"We're staying in the Gate House Cottage at the Mabel Dodge Luhan House," Antonio replied.

Rodgers nodded and wrote that down in a small notebook.

Fernando and Antonio watched as one of the deputies went to get a stretcher from the Forensics van. Then two deputies put the unsightly body in a body bag and then carried it up to the van and loaded it in the rear.

After Forensics and the sheriff's deputies cleared out, Fernando pointed to a picnic table under a tall Ponderosa pine. "Let's talk."

Antonio followed him over to the picnic table and sat across from Fernando. "As soon as you get the death certificate and the mortuary takes possession of the body, I'm heading back to Santa Fe. I don't know, maybe if you arrange for some kind of ceremony at Jesus Nazareno I'll come up for that. Maybe Manny might want to come along, just to close that chapter."

"Yeah, well, I'm eager to get back home to Alamosa too, but there's one other thing we have to do before we can leave," Antonio said, frowning. He looked dead serious.

"What's that?"

"Payback," Antonio replied. "You don't think I'm gonna let Daniel and fucking Art Stokes get away with what they did to Jack, do you?"

"Payback?" Fernando asked, almost pleading.

"Payback!" Antonio said and smashed his palm down on the picnic table so hard the flimsy table shook like a wet dog.

23

Fernando was afraid to ask what Antonio had in mind. What kind of payback? Now that Lacy's body had been found again, he wanted to head back to Santa Fe as soon as possible, if not sooner. The last thing he wanted was to get involved in some messy shootout with Art Stokes, or whatever Antonio had in mind. From all appearances Stokes was bat shit crazy. Liable to do anything.

"Come on, let's get it over with," Antonio said. "You can stay in the Cherokee if you don't want to participate, but I want to care take of this right away, while I'm still in the mood."

"In the mood?" Fernando asked, slightly amused by Antonio's phrasing. "What do you mean by in the mood? Angry?"

Antonio waved him off and started walking back to the Cherokee. Fernando followed, shaking his head. They climbed into the Cherokee without speaking, at a standoff.

Fernando fired up the big engine and pulled out on Highway 68 north. He drove through Taos and then, against his better judgment, turned right on Highway 150 to Arroyo Seco. He clung to the hope that Stokes wouldn't be at home—that he would be out spending his ten thousand dollars with his buddy Daniel. He looked like the kind of guy who would spend whatever money came his way as fast as he could spend it, or faster.

As they turned into Stokes' driveway they saw his two-tone van parked in front of the dilapidated house and Fernando's spirits sank. He parked behind the van and let Antonio take the lead. This was his play.

Fernando saw his role as providing some semblance of restraint. He would try his damnedest to keep Antonio from killing or seriously injuring Stokes—who, after all, was a tiny old man.

Antonio walked up to the torn screen door and flung it open. Then he walked through the open door into the front room, where Daniel sat on the sofa calmly, unruffled by Antonio's aggression.

"Where's Stokes?" Antonio asked.

"Not here," Daniel said.

"Where is he?" Antonio demanded.

Daniel pointed to the kitchen door. "Outside."

Antonio walked through the kitchen and out the door. Fernando followed, staying back a few steps.

Once outside they spotted Stokes coming up out of the root cellar carrying a glass jar. Stokes stopped dead in his tracks when he saw Antonio approaching. For just a moment a look of fear flickered on the old man's face. Fear at seeing the big man coming at him with murder in his eyes.

"Hey—get off my property!" Stokes shouted, trying his best to regroup. He dropped the glass jar, which shattered on a slab of flagstone outside the door of the root cellar. "Leave me the hell alone!"

"You think that was funny, what you did back at the bridge?" Antonio asked. "You ever hear of gross abuse of a corpse? I oughta have you arrested and thrown in jail."

"Get out of here, you big sonofabitch!" Stokes sputtered. He fumbled a moment and then pulled a pistol out of his waistband.

A big mistake.

Instantly Antonio pounced on Stokes, wrestling the pistol out of the old man's hand and then backhanding him. Stokes fell backwards and landed flat on his ass in the dirt. Antonio then marched over to the wooden outhouse and opened the flimsy door. Laughing at Stokes, he dropped the gun into the nearest hole in the seat and listened for the splat.

Antonio turned back to Stokes. "If you want your gun back, you can crawl down the hole and wallow around in your shit!"

"Goddamn you!" Stokes yelled and charged Antonio, flailing away with both hands. Smiling, Antonio stiff-armed the emaciated old man with his left hand, keeping him at a safe distance.

Finally Antonio tired of the hysterics. He grabbed Stokes by the waist and flung him over his shoulder in one quick motion.

"Let me down, you fucker!" Stokes screamed, pounding on Antonio's back with both hands.

"Hit me one more time and I'll stuff you down the same shit hole in the outhouse I threw your gun into," Antonio barked, after which Stokes stopped hitting Antonio's back.

Antonio snorted and carried the old man like a sack of grain across the dirt yard to the tumbledown wooden corral, where Stokes' two scraggly cows watched them approach with sad, hollow eyes. Fernando followed, worried about what Antonio was about to do.

"Oww! Put me down!" Stokes screamed again.

"Open the gate for me," Antonio said to Fernando, once they came closer to the corral.

"My pleasure," Fernando said, suddenly realizing what Antonio intended to do with Stokes.

Antonio carried Stokes over to the round water tank. With a depth of three or four feet and a diameter of about eight feet, the metal tank was filled with green slimy water and a couple of frogs who jumped out when they saw Antonio approach with his human cargo, kicking and screaming on his back.

Without hesitating, Antonio pitched Stokes into the water with a big splash. Stokes came sputtering up out of the water, gasping for air, but Antonio pushed his head back under the green slime.

"Should I drown the old bastard?" Antonio asked.

"No! You've made your point," Fernando said, not wanting Antonio to do something he would regret.

Antonio took his hand away and Stokes shot up out of the slimy water again, coughing loudly, trying to get the water out of his lungs.

Fernando grabbed Antonio's arm. "Enough...let's go."

Antonio nodded and stepped back, allowing Stokes to splash to the other side of the tank, as far away from Antonio as he could get. The little man tried to crawl out of the slimy tank but slipped while trying to climb over the top rim and pitched head first in the dirt yard.

"Oww!" Stokes howled loudly. He grabbed on to the top of the tank and managed to pull himself up to a standing position, his hands and face covered with brown mud. He let loose a string a profanity while attempting to wipe the mud off his face with his shirt sleeves.

Antonio ignored Stokes. Instead, he walked slowly out of the corral with a big smile on his face.

Fernando followed. He noticed Daniel standing near the fence on the far side of the corral watching them. His face was blank. Not a trace of emotion or interest of any kind. Blank.

Fernando walked up to Daniel and asked, "Do you want a ride to your sister's house?"

Daniel shook his head. "No."

Fernando nodded. "Whatever you say." He noticed the two placid cows watching him as he walked out of the corral, leaving the gate wide open so the cows could decide whether they wanted to stay or hit the open mesa. They might have better luck foraging on the mesa than waiting for Stokes to feed them.

Antonio was waiting for him at the Cherokee, already sitting in the passenger seat buckled in. He started laughing and slapping his legs.

"Happy now?" Fernando asked, climbing into the driver's seat.

"Pretty damn," Antonio replied. "Doesn't make up for what he did to Jack, but it's a taste of his own medicine."

"Did you happen to see Daniel watching from the other side of the corral?" Fernando asked.

"I did, yes. He's a weird bird," Antonio tossed off. "He doesn't talk much, does he?"

Fernando started the Cherokee and drove off down the dusty driveway. Once they got back on the highway, Antonio asked, "You want to stop at Orlando's for lunch and a beer?"

Fernando shook his head. "No, I need to get back to Santa Fe. Estelle is really pissed."

"Aren't you going to stay for the burial?"

"Sorry, Antonio, I just can't stay any longer," Fernando replied. Seeing the big man's disappointment, he added, "I'll tell you what I'll do. Call me when you have a date for the burial. I'll try to come back. Like I said, maybe I can even convince Manny to come with me."

Antonio nodded but did not respond.

Just then Fernando heard a ping on his phone. He glanced at his phone in his front pocket and saw the text was from Estelle. He ignored it for the time being, negotiating the curves leading out of Arroyo Seco.

After turning on Highway 64 Fernando looked for a place to pull over. He found it when Overland Ranch came into view, so he turned left into the big parking lot and put the Cherokee in Park while he read Estelle's text.

He expected Estelle to berate him about staying too long in Taos and to demand that he return to Santa Fe immediately. Instead, he was surprised to read: "Fernando, I am getting a lot done while you're in Taos. Enjoying myself. Stay as long as you want. Estelle."

24

Was Estelle serious? Was she being sarcastic? What? Fernando couldn't decide. All he knew was that it wasn't like Estelle to tell him to stay away for as long as he wanted. Maybe she'd given up on trying to rein him in. Or, worse case scenario, maybe she'd decided to kick him out of the house as soon as he returned. Goodbye Fernando! These and other depressing thoughts kept popping up in his mind as he turned into the big parking lot at the Luhan House and parked beside Antonio's Wrangler. Horror of horrors, what had he done?

"What's wrong with you now?" Antonio asked, as they climbed out of the Cherokee.

Fernando showed the mysterious text to Antonio, who glared at the phone for several moments before speaking. "What's the problem? She's giving you a blank check, right?" Antonio asked.

"I don't know—I think she's really pissed this time," Fernando replied. "I'm worried about what she'll do."

"Look at the bright side, now you can stay in Taos and help with the funeral arrangements," Antonio said.

The bright side? Fernando didn't think so.

They walked into the Gate House Cottage, which again seemed somehow deserted without Lacy lying in the bedroom. Fernando collapsed on the sofa while Antonio headed for the bedroom. "I need to check in with my son in Alamosa," Antonio said. "I kinda left him in the lurch. We were late starting baling season. When I left he was trying to find some temporary hands to help finish the job, which aren't easy to find in Alamosa."

Antonio opened the door to the patio and sat down at the table, taking his cell phone out of his shirt pocket and speed dialing.

Fernando sat back on the sofa, feeling exhausted. He listened to

Antonio talking to his son for a few minutes and then decided to take a nap. His eyelids felt heavy; he couldn't keep his eyes open. When he laid back on the sofa he saw Antonio come back into the bedroom and lie down on the big bed. He couldn't remember ever seeing Antonio take a nap. Both of them were played out. Too much running around. Too much stress.

As soon as he closed his eyes the dream began. He found himself standing at dusk along a dark river under a darkening sky. He heard water splashing. Like a great beast emerging from the water, a tall thin man stomped out of the river. In the fading light Fernando saw the grim figure approach with water pouring from his body. The man's bare abdomen was bloated and marked with darkly colored splotches. His face, if he had one, was lost in the darkness. He stopped a few feet away and, still dripping water, reached out a hand to Fernando, who cringed back when he saw the bony fingers of a skeleton.

The man with no face spoke slowly, solemnly. "See before you another lost soul...blocked from fully crossing over by violent death... now abandoned by those on the other side...doomed to wander alone until his murder is revenged and the balance restored...."

Fernando awoke in a cold sweat. He struggled to sit up. He heard Antonio talking in the bedroom. He sat on the sofa for a few moments trying to wake up from whatever he just experienced—a dream, a nightmare, a vision, or a visitation of some sort, he had no idea. Then he walked into the bedroom and found Antonio sitting on the edge of the bed shaking his head. He seemed troubled.

"Shit! That's why I don't take naps," Antonio said.

"What do you mean?" Fernando asked.

"I saw Jack," Antonio replied. "He was walking out of the river and talking about violent death—his violent death. What the fuck?"

Shocked, Fernando collapsed in the Queen Anne chair next to the bed. He didn't know what to say, or think. Should he tell Antonio he'd seen the same thing? Was that a real visitation or were they both losing it?

Antonio noticed Fernando's confusion. "What's your problem? You look sick, like you're about to throw up."

"I saw the same thing," Fernando said. "He walked right out of the river and said he'd been blocked from fully crossing over by a violent death. But how? He died from Glioblastoma."

"Maybe Glioblastoma is what he meant by a violent death," Antonio offered.

Fernando shook his head. "I don't think so. He talked about not being able to cross until his murder is revenged."

Antonio stared at Fernando, not responding.

Later they migrated out to the patio and continued to avoid talking about their shared vision. Neither of them knew what to say or how to make sense of the coincidence, if it was a coincidence. Soon it became too late for Fernando to head back to Santa Fe. Might as well stay another night. Didn't Estelle tell him to stay as long as he wanted? Or did she mean the opposite under a layer of sarcasm? She sometimes used sarcasm as a way to deliver her edicts indirectly. He couldn't decide what she meant or if and when to leave for Santa Fe.

Eventually, just as they started to talk about going to dinner, they heard a car pull up to the Gate House Cottage. When someone knocked on the door Fernando wondered if Manny had come back to get more information. He let Antonio answer the door and was surprised to see Deputy Sheriff Rodgers outside on the porch. "Sure, come in," Antonio said to Rodgers.

Rodgers stepped inside and nodded to Fernando and Antonio. The tall, muscular Rodgers looked around the front room. "Nice...I've never been inside the Gate House Cottage."

"Yeah...I like it better than the big house," Antonio said. "Spooky up there. Especially Mabel's bedroom."

"No kidding," Rodgers said. "Did they tell you about the ghosts up at the office? Paranormal organizations around town have made recordings of the ghosts. Some believe it, some don't."

Antonio laughed. "I hear you. I used to be a nonbeliever, but now I'm not so sure."

"Well, the reason I stopped by was to give you a copy of Jack Lacy's death certificate," Rodgers said, handing the document to Antonio. "Also I need you to sign some papers so we can pass along the body to Rivera Family Funerals. You can just write family friend where it asks for your relationship to the deceased. I assume you're not family?"

Antonio nodded. He signed the papers and handed them back. Then he noticed something on the death certificate. "Wait—this lists the cause of death as Glioblastoma slash suffocation. What's that all about?"

"Yeah, I wanted to talk to you about that," Rodgers replied, stroking his chin. "Forensics found damage to Lacy's neck, damage caused by fingers digging into the neck tissue. In addition, Lacy's larynx was crushed. Whoever grabbed him around the neck had very strong fingers."

Fernando stepped up to join the conversation, interested now. "Could this have occurred when the body was in the river, bumping against rocks as it went through the rapids?"

Rodgers shook his head. "No...not with the finger indentations. It's from someone choking him."

"Jesus!" Antonio said, glancing at Fernando. "So you're talking about murder then?"

"Well...maybe...they're just not sure," Rodgers said. "Thing is, Forensics couldn't determine exactly when the choking occurred—when Lacy was still alive, or just after he died. They thought about sending the body down to the state Medical Examiner's office in Albuquerque, which is better equipped to make that determination. But that would be expensive and could take weeks, so Forensics and the sheriff decided it wasn't worth the extra time and expense, since Lacy was dying or already dead when the choking occurred. That's why the cause of death is listed as Glioblastoma slash suffocation."

Antonio nodded. "Okay...thanks. I'll make arrangements for the funeral and burial once Rivera gets the body."

"Good enough," Rodgers said. "I'll let Forensics know."

With that, Rodgers turned and quickly made his way out of the Gate House Cottage, leaving Antonio and Fernando standing in the front room staring in silence at each other.

"Daniel!" both of them said at the same time.

25

As soon as Deputy Sheriff Rodgers left, Fernando and Antonio locked up the Gate House Cottage and climbed into the Cherokee. Fernando drove down to Kit Carson Road and once again headed to Luz's house. It was high time to confront Luz and Daniel about Lacy's injury. They wanted an explanation. Even more, they wanted to know if Luz, a practicing crossover curandera, could rectify the matter so that Lacy could cross over and join the ghost of Dennis Hopper, as he wished. There must be something she could do with all her other-worldly knowledge, her chants and potions. At least that's what Fernando hoped.

"This is on fucking Luz—and she better be able to fix the problem," Antonio said, angry once again. Sometimes it seemed to Fernando that angry was Antonio's natural state of mind.

"Yeah, well, don't forget brother Daniel," Fernando replied. "He's the one who must have done this. I can't imagine tiny old Art Stokes having a strong enough grip to cause Lacy's larynx to collapse. He's a wimp!"

"Can't you go any faster?" Antonio kept asking as Fernando cruised along Kit Carson Road.

In response Fernando took his foot off the accelerator and slowed down. "Listen, calm down. You have to stay cool. I don't want you running into the house and busting heads before we even get an explanation of why this happened and how we can fix it...okay?"

Antonio let loose a string of profanity that convinced Fernando to pull over on the side of Kit Carson Road. "I'm not going any further until I know I can count on you to act rationally...professionally. Pretend you're still a police sergeant—that your job is to enforce the law, not take it into your own hands. Okay?"

"I knew I should have fucking driven," Antonio shot back.

They sat there with the engine turned off for several minutes. Finally Antonio seemed to calm down, so Fernando fired up the engine again and continued down to Highway 585. This time when they pulled into Luz's driveway she was nowhere to be seen, not on the front porch and not on the trails of the foothills behind her house. Fortunately her vehicle was parked in the driveway.

Fernando parked off to the side of the wrap-around porch. Antonio jumped out of the Cherokee and darted up on the porch before Fernando could even unbuckle his seatbelt and climb out of the driver's seat. "Wait for me...." Fernando called out, as Antonio opened the front door and disappeared into the house without bothering to knock.

Cursing, Fernando hurried after Antonio. When he stepped inside he could hear Antonio's booming voice: "Where's Daniel? Did you help him murder Jack Lacy? So you could get your money?"

Fernando hurried into the kitchen. He found Luz now wearing an apron over her purple dress and standing over a stove stirring pots on all four burners. On the counter next to the stove sat a collection of mason jars filled with herbs. Some of the labels he recognized: Lavender, Gold Weed, Hollyhock, Comfrey, Stinkweed, and Verbena. Others he didn't.

Antonio moved closer to Luz, towering over the woman. Luz was a tall, packed woman, but next to Antonio she looked petite.

"Careful, I'm making teas and potions," Luz said. "You need to stand back. These are scalding hot."

Her composure amazed Fernando. She didn't seem to be threatened or even bothered by the big man's rage.

"Now...tell me, what's all this anger about?" Luz asked, after Antonio took a step back. She eyed Antonio and said, "You do know that anger is detrimental to your health? It takes a terrible toll on your heart and lungs. It's a silent killer."

"We were given Jack Lacy's death certificate this afternoon," Fernando jumped in, figuring he better take the lead in order to keep Antonio from exploding. "Turns out the cause of his death was both Glioblastoma and suffocation. Someone choked him hard enough to crush his larynx. Someone with very strong fingers. This happened here in your house, on your watch."

A look of concern flashed on Luz's face. She looked worried now. She turned off the burners on the stove and then removed her apron and calmly hung it on a hook near the refrigerator.

"Well...I left the body here when I went to Albertsons to get flowers," she said. "The body was gone when I got back."

"You left the body with Daniel and his friend, Art Stokes!" Antonio barked. "Stokes doesn't have the strength in his hands to crush someone's larynx. Where's Daniel?"

Luz glanced at the hallway.

"Where is he?" Fernando added.

They followed Luz into the long workroom, with the masseuse table at one end and the crossover bed Lacy had occupied at the other end. At first the room appeared deserted, but then Luz pointed to the exercise mats on the other side of the masseuse table where Daniel was lifting weights. Lying flat on his back, Daniel was stretching his back and lifting small hand weights.

"Daniel, I need to ask you something important," Luz said in a calm, friendly voice. She smiled at Daniel.

Without responding, Daniel stopped lifting weights and looked at Luz. When he sat up, he noticed Fernando and Antonio behind Luz and suddenly bolted to his feet. He stood staring at them, fists balled.

"I want you to tell me the truth, Daniel," Luz said. "When I left you with Mister Lacy, did you choke him?"

Daniel made a funny noise, like a little yelp. He stared at his sister for a long moment and then said, "I helped him cross. He was having trouble. He kept saying, 'I can't do it. I can't do it.' So I helped him."

Luz, Fernando, and Antonio all stared at Daniel. No one spoke. The silence was deafening.

Finally Antonio threw up his hands and turned away without speaking. He walked into the hallway and then changed his mind and came back into the workroom. He stood there for a few seconds and then turned away and again walked into the hallway. This time he kept going, walking out the front door of the house. They heard the big man sit heavily on the porch swing and the yawning of the swing moving back and forth, back and forth.

Relieved that Antonio hadn't exploded and hurt either Luz or Daniel, Fernando stepped forward and said, "So then Lacy was still alive when you left," Fernando said to Luz.

"His heart must have been fluttering," Luz said calmly. "He was fading in and out of consciousness. I couldn't feel a pulse or see him breathing before I left. He was either dead or dying."

Fernando nodded. He believed Luz. She had no reason not to tell the truth about what happened.

"So at any rate Mister Lacy was dead, or in the process of dying and would have been dead within in minutes, when Daniel helped him cross over," Luz said. "I hope you take that into consideration before you do something that would have dire consequences for my brother. He was only trying to help."

"I do realize that," Fernando replied. "Here's the problem we have now. Lacy appeared to both Antonio and I in visions saying that he's blocked from fully crossing over because of his violent death. So what can we do now to get him across? How can we unblock him?"

Luz thought for a moment. She nodded. "Okay...we can fix this. I'll do a crossover ceremony for someone who is lost or simply not present. For that ceremony I will need a photograph of Mister Lacy and some of his clothes or belongings. Clothes would be better. Can you provide those?"

"Yes, I have his passport and suitcase back at the Gate House Cottage," Antonio said. "I can go get them."

Luz smiled "Good. Why don't you bring them later, about five o'clock. Sundown is the perfect time for this ceremony. That will give me time to do the other ceremony I need to do with Daniel."

"What kind of ceremony is that?" Fernando asked.

"A ceremony to absolve and cleanse him for what he did to Mister Lacy," Luz replied. "It needs to be done first, before I do the crossover ceremony for Mister Lacy. Daniel will have to be healed first."

Fernando shook his head. Would that it were that easy to absolve someone of murder.

"Okay, whatever it takes," Fernando said. "Just get it done."

26

Back at the Gate House Cottage Antonio threw open the patio doors for fresh air and then carried Lacy's suitcase over to the big bed. He unzipped the black carry-on and rummaged through its contents. In the side pocket he found Lacy's passport and other valuables, including a wallet, two sets of keys, and a Rolex watch. He picked up the Rolex and held it out for Fernando to see. "Want a Rolex watch?" Antonio asked. "Too rich for my blood."

Fernando shook his head. "Mine too. Plus Ruby and Blaine and the Canyon Road crowd would give me a hard time about wearing a dead man's watch. Being on dead man's time."

Antonio laughed. "Yes, they would. I can hear them now, especially Ruby with her sharp tongue."

"What else do you see in the suitcase?" Fernando asked.

"Mostly clothes so far," Antonio said, still rummaging in the suitcase. "He already gave me his credit cards and the checkbook with the five hundred grand. I have his pistol locked in the glove compartment of the Wrangler. Took some convincing before Jack would give me the gun. He once told me he felt naked when he wasn't armed."

"I can believe it," Fernando said. "He loved his guns. He was the best marksman I ever saw. Could shoot a hair off a man's chin."

"Ah, hell, I'll just take the whole damn suitcase," Antonio said, tossing everything he'd taken out back into the suitcase and zipping it closed. "Better to let Luz decide—I don't know what she needs."

Fernando checked his watch. "Let's hit the road, even if we're a little early. I don't know why it would matter."

Antonio put Lacy's passport in his back pocket and grabbed the suitcase. "The sooner the better. I'm tired of dealing with this."

Fernando followed Antonio outside to the Wrangler. The big man tossed the suitcase in the rear compartment and climbed into the driver's seat. Fernando rode shotgun.

They arrived at Luz's house thirty minutes early. When they walked into the house Luz was still setting up. They found her in the workroom arranging candles and incense on the long table beside the bed. In addition to the beads, amulets, and crosses they'd seen before, Luz had several bunches of herbs and flowers scattered around the table and the floor. For some reason her brother Daniel sat quietly in a chair at the foot of the bed. Daniel had his eyes closed, as if he were meditating.

Antonio scowled when he saw Daniel sitting at the foot of the bed. "What's he doing here?"

"We just finished Daniel's cleansing ceremony," Luz replied. "You're a little early."

"Hah! Cleansing ceremony my ass!" Antonio spit out. "I'll show you how to cleanse him."

After opening his eyes, Daniel turned his head away and refused to look at Antonio.

"Look at me, you piece of shit!" Antonio barked and then grabbed Daniel around the neck with his huge right hand that was as big as a baseball glove. "Let's see how you like it when I crush your larynx!"

Both Fernando and Luz rushed to stop Antonio. Fernando grabbed Antonio's arm, while Luz tried to pry off Antonio's fingers gripping Daniel's neck. "Please...stop...we need peace to perform the ceremony," Luz pleaded.

Fernando and Luz managed to remove Antonio's hand, which left Daniel bent over and coughing violently, trying to get his breath.

Fernando put his arm around Antonio's shoulders. "Come on, let's go outside and cool off," he said, trying to escort Antonio out of the room. Antonio resisted at first but finally relented and went with Fernando. They walked outside to the porch and sat together on the porch swing.

"Sorry...I lost it," Antonio said.

"No problem. I understand," Fernando said. "It's been a long ordeal, but we're almost finished now. One more ceremony to help Lacy cross over and then we're done. Why don't you wait out here on the porch. I'll make sure Luz does everything she can to help Lacy cross over. Okay?"

Antonio nodded. "Okay, but keep that piece of shit away from me. If I see him again, I just might kill him with my own hands."

"No problem, I'll keep him inside," Fernando said. He patted Antonio on the back and then went back inside, where Luz and Daniel were standing together at the foot of the bed waiting for him.

Fernando spoke to Luz, ignoring Daniel. "You need to keep your brother away from Antonio. If Antonio sees him again, I don't know that I can stop him. You have no idea how strong Antonio is...no idea."

Luz nodded and gave Daniel instructions to go into her bedroom down the hall and shelter in the closet until she came to get him." Daniel agreed and, still rubbing his neck, tiptoed quietly out of the room and down the hallway. They heard the door of her bedroom close.

"Okay, then. Let's get this over with," Fernando said. "I'm running out of patience."

Luz nodded. She looked around the room. "Oh, good, you brought Mister Lacy's belongings," Luz said when she saw the suitcase Antonio had carried in. "Did you bring the photograph?"

"Antonio has it," Fernando said. "I'll be right back."

"Yes, because I need a photo...."

Fernando went out to the patio where Antonio was still sitting on the porch swing. "I'll need Lacy's passport for the ceremony,"

Antonio took the passport out of his back pocket and passed it to Fernando. "Hurry up...I'm losing my patience."

Fernando took the passport back inside and handed it to Luz, who opened the passport and laid it on the pillow at the top of the bed, so that the photo of Lacy was visible.

"Perfect," Luz said, standing back to get a better view.

Then Luz unzipped Lacy's suitcase and placed it on the bed. She pawed through the contents of the suitcase, taking out a shirt and a pair of trousers. She arranged them on the bed as if Lacy was lying on the bed wearing the clothes. It took her several minutes to get all the details just right. Meanwhile, Fernando stood at the foot of the bed waiting impatiently for the ceremony to begin. When Luz placed the suitcase on the floor under the bed, he knew she was finally ready.

"Okay, let's begin with a moment of silence," Luz said, lowering her head. First she lit a large candle on the table. Then she turned and addressed Lacy, or his photograph, directly. She told him this was the moment of saying farewell to life and his friends and loved ones. She told him the light from the candle represents the light of the Spirit who was present at that very moment and who would accompany him on his journey to the spirit world.

At that point Luz paused a moment and closed her eyes. When she opened them again she began speaking in broad generalities, talking about the interconnectivity of all human consciousness, that we are all connected to the consciousness of those who came before us and those who will come after us. "Now as your road comes to an end, walk into the light," she said.

After pausing for a long moment with her eyes closed, Luz finished the ceremony by reciting a prayer:

"Now leave your body
And let your spirit soar.
See the pure light of the evening sun.
Follow it and travel on your own road.
May every day be a bridge between yesterday and tomorrow.
May you live in connection to those who came before you
And those who will come after you.
May you live in connection to your soul
And listen to the voice of silence.
May peace be with you always."

With that, Luz extinguished the candle on the bedside table. She turned to Fernando and nodded. "That should do it," she said. "He should be free and able to cross over."

Fernando held his tongue. As a materialist, he remained skeptical of her high-flying language. Still, if her ceremony freed Lacy and kept him out of Fernando and Antonio's dreams, then all the better. He almost felt like hugging Luz. Would that be appropriate? He decided it would not.

"So are we done?" Fernando asked.

Luz nodded. "We're done."

Fernando lingered for a while near the bed and then grabbed Lacy's clothes and put them back in the suitcase. He tucked Lacy's passport in his back pocket and then stood looking at Luz, as if he didn't know what else to say. Finally he said, "Okay, then...I hope you're right."

Luz nodded. "Not to worry."

Fernando paused before leaving. "I'm on my way back to Santa Fe, so I guess this is a long goodbye. I can't say it's been pleasant, but it's certainly been educational, I will say that."

Luz smiled broadly.

Then he turned and walked out of the room and down the long hallway carrying the suitcase. The front door stood wide open. Looked like Antonio might have damaged it when he opened it and then slammed it against the wall. Fernando stepped through the open door and found Antonio still sitting in the porch swing. Antonio jumped up out of the swing as soon as he saw Fernando. Neither of them spoke as they climbed down off the porch and walked to the Wrangler. Antonio fired up the engine and drove back onto the highway. When they reached the Gate House Cottage, they went inside, still without speaking.

Once inside, Antonio turned to Fernando and asked, "So what do you think? Did the ceremony work?"

Fernando shrugged. "I have no idea. I know nothing about any of this. If the ceremony works, it works."

"I guess we'll know it worked if Lacy stops appearing in our dreams," Antonio replied.

"I guess."

"Are you still going back to Santa Fe today?" Antonio asked.

Fernando nodded. "Yeah...I'm in enough trouble with Estelle now. Like I said, let me know when Lacy's funeral or burial is scheduled and I'll try to come back. Maybe bring Manny with me."

"I'm not planning on a funeral," Antonio said. "Maybe we'll say a few words at the burial in Jesus Nazareno, we'll see."

"Sounds right. I think Jack would like that," Fernando said.

Antonio sat on the sofa and watched while Fernando packed his duffle, which he'd only bothered to bring into the cottage this morning. It didn't take long to pack, because other than underwear he hadn't changed his clothes since arriving at the Luhan House.

On his way to the front door Fernando stopped, seeing Antonio sitting idly on the sofa, looking forlorn.

Fernando walked back to Antonio and gave him a bear hug.

Antonio smiled.

Vaya con dios," Fernando said and turned away. On his way out the kitchen door he realized he hadn't uttered that expression in years.

Why now?

27

The long drive back to Santa Fe gave Fernando time to reflect on the events of the last few days. Though he had never been a fan of Jack Lacy's, he admired Antonio's dedication to his old war buddy, including Antonio's determination to help Lacy through his last days on earth. He realized, driving down the dark lonesome highway, that he and Antonio would do the same for each other. Except for Estelle, Antonio had been the best friend he'd ever had. The thought of never seeing Antonio again after Lacy's burial filled him with sadness. What would he do without the comfort of knowing Antonio was always there for him?

He pulled into his driveway on Acequia Madre Street about 9:30 p.m. totally exhausted. His house was dark, unusual for this early in the evening. He parked behind Estelle's Camry and walked up to the porch, unlocked the door, and stepped inside the dark kitchen. For a moment he considered foraging in the refrigerator for something to eat since he hadn't eaten much all day, but then decided against it. He was too damned tired to do anything but sleep.

Fernando disrobed in the kitchen and tossed his dirty clothes in the laundry room. Not only were the clothes filthy, they stank to high heaven because he'd worn them every day in Taos, too lazy to change. Over the years he'd perfected the art of disrobing in the kitchen or living room when he'd come home late and dirty, hoping Estelle wouldn't notice his late return. Then, wearing only his underwear, he tiptoed down the hallway to the bedroom and crawled into bed with Estelle. He congratulated himself on not waking Estelle. Until she rolled over and whispered, "About time."

That night he dreamed repeatedly of a crossover ceremony. He found himself in a dark room where the only light came from feeble candles situated on what looked like an altar from a Catholic church.

A priest or curandera fluttered around the altar, tending the candles and administering to a human form on a bed. The human's face was lost in the darkness as the shaman-figure chanted and prayed while waving a burning pot of incense over the prone figure. The shaman-figure wore a mask, not a Native American mask but a cheap plastic werewolf mask like he wore for Halloween when he was a kid. Finished with chanting and praying, the shaman-figure put down the pot of incense and picked up a candle, passing it back and forth over the figure on the bed. As the candle moved it revealed more of the face of the man on the bed. The face didn't look like Lacy's—too round with a heavy chin. The candle kept moving, revealing more and more of the face until Fernando realized he was looking at his own face. He was lying on that bed about to cross over!

"No! Stop! Not me! I'm not ready to cross over!" he screamed in his dream, waving his hands.

Fernando awoke in a cold sweat, his feet thrashing in the bedclothes. Estelle yelped and then said, "What's the matter?"

"Nightmare," he mumbled.

"Maybe you should go back to Taos," Estelle said and then a moment later added, "I'm just kidding!"

Fernando laughed. Sort of. "That's where I got the nightmare. I don't want to go back."

"Well, don't tell me about it...I don't want to know, because if you do tell me I'll probably start having the same nightmare," Estelle said and crawled out of bed.

After Estelle left the bed, Fernando glanced at the clock on the nightstand and saw that it was already morning. He'd slept all night, like a dead man.

Fernando stayed in bed while Estelle slipped on her robe and went into the kitchen. He heard her making coffee and then breakfast. Wary of her mood, he took his time getting out of bed and dressing. Then he walked down the long hall to the kitchen, feeling as though he were walking to his execution.

He was surprised to find the kitchen table set for two and a cheese and green chile omelet on each plate, alongside a steaming cup of coffee. When he sat in his usual chair at the table, Estelle came around behind him and surprised him again by kissing him on the neck.

"I'm glad you're home," Estelle said. "But you're not totally off the hook—I'm still mad that you didn't call to let me know what was going on."

Fernando smiled and pleaded guilty. "I know. I should have contacted you. Sorry about that. Things just got crazy up there."

"So tell me about it now," Estelle said, sitting across from him in her usual place at the table.

So Fernando told her about Jack Lacy, Antonio's old war buddy, who was dying of Glioblastoma and wanted to be buried close to his old friend Dennis Hopper in Jesus Nazareno Cemetery in Ranchos de Taos. He mentioned that Lacy had hired a curandera to help him cross over and that his body was kidnapped right after the ceremony and then tossed off the Rio Grande Gorge Bridge into the Rio Grande by the kidnappers. He tried to end the sad, morbid tale on a positive note, saying the body was recovered and currently being prepared for burial in a day or so, an event that he might have to attend in order to see Antonio one last time before he returned to Alamosa to help his son with their ranch.

Estelle stared at him as if he were bonkers. "That's just about the craziest story I've ever heard. Tossed off the Rio Grande Gorge Bridge? Who are these people? Who would do something like that?"

So Fernando told her about Daniel and Art Stokes.

"What about the crossover ceremony?" Estelle asked. "Did you actually attend one?"

Fernando nodded. "Two of them, actually. The first one to help Lacy cross over and the second one to get him unblocked."

"Unblocked? What do you mean?" Estelle asked.

Fernando tried to explain how Lacy's violent death—being choked by the curandera's brother—had prevented him from crossing, so a second crossover ceremony had to be held in order to unblock him. He didn't tell her about Lacy's ghost or spirit visiting both him and Antonio in their dreams, for fear that Estelle would think he'd gone off the deep end.

After listening to Fernando's bizarre tale, Estelle just shook her head. "Taos...I don't know why you keep going back there."

"Thing is, I can't shake the feeling that I'll never see Antonio again," Fernando said. "I'm losing him. I'm losing my best friend...he's been like a blood brother to me. Like the brother I never had."

"Well, then, let's go up for his friend Lacy's burial, I'll come along with you," Estelle said. "And you can always drive up to visit him in Alamosa, it's not that long of a drive."

So it was decided. The two of them would attend the ceremony at Lacy's burial in Jesus Nazareno.

After breakfast Estelle showered and left for work at the immigrant outreach program. Fernando made himself another cup of coffee and took it outside to the patio, where he did his best thinking. Or brooding. Having Estelle accompany him to Taos for Lacy's burial would limit what he and Antonio could do in terms of celebrating. Maybe that would be for the best. It would give him a reason to go visit Antonio, maybe next Spring. He didn't much like leaving the state anymore, but Alamosa wasn't very much farther than Taos.

After a third cup of coffee Fernando decided to go for a walk on Acequia Madre Street. Walking was the one form of exercise he tolerated. Every other form of physical exercise bored him to death. At least when walking he could continue to brood. Face it, he was a brooder.

He locked up the house and then took his time walking to the end of Acequia Madre. The leaves on some of the trees along the street were starting to turn. Soon the aspen and cottonwood leaves would sparkle yellow in the sun. He liked the autumn colors and the smell of piñon wood burning in the fireplaces along the street. The only problem with fall was that it led into winter, his least favorite season. Given its elevation, Santa Fe was damn cold during the winter.

On the way back to his house a text pinged on his phone. He stopped walking and read the text, from Antonio: "Lacy's burial will be tomorrow at 1 o'clock. With music and a small gathering. Hope you can come."

So it was set, the final act in the Lacy tragedy, if you wanted to call it a tragedy. Fernando decided to call Manny at the Washington Avenue Station as soon as he got home to see if Manny wanted to ride along with them to Taos for Lacy's burial. They'd talked about it briefly in Taos.

He didn't bother to open the kitchen door and go inside. Instead, he sat on the patio again and took his cell phone out of his pocket. When he called, Manny answered immediately, as usual.

"Fernando, what's up? Are you back in Santa Fe?" Manny asked.

"Got back last night," Fernando said. "You can tell the Chief that if he wants to arrest Jack Lacy for murdering Tom Hammond, then he'll have to drive up to Jesus Nazareno Cemetery in Ranchos de Taos and dig up Lacy's body."

Manny laughed. "I'd like to see that—the Chief digging up the grave and actually doing some physical work instead of just lecturing the rest of us for what we failed to do or did wrong."

"How well I remember," Fernando said. "The one thing the Chief was good at—lecturing."

"So Lacy passed, then? That's good, I guess, under the circumstances," Manny said.

"Yeah...and the burial is tomorrow at one o'clock in Jesus Nazareno Cemetery," Fernando replied. "You said you might want to attend. You want to come along with us—Estelle is coming too, if that makes a difference."

"Sure, no, it's fine that Estelle's coming," Manny said. "I get along with her a lot better than I get along with you," he said, laughing.

Fernando laughed too. "I know. She'll be a buffer so that the two of us don't get into it."

"Exactly."

"So why don't you come over here about eleven o'clock or so," Fernando said. "That should give us plenty of time."

"I'll be there," Manny said. "It'll be good to see Antonio again before he goes back to Colorado. Oops, here comes the Chief. See you tomorrow."

Before going into the house, Fernando used his cell phone to Google the distance from Taos to Alamosa. Turned out to be only 90 miles, via Highways 64 and 285 North. A mere one hour and thirty-seven minutes, according to Google. Maybe late May or early June would be a good time to visit. He smiled, already planning his trip and what all he would take with him.

Surely they sold Modelo in southern Colorado?

28

They arrived at Jesus Nazareno Cemetery a few minutes before one o'clock. Fernando saw the Rivera Family Funeral Home hearse as he pulled into the small parking lot. He parked at the end of the line of cars, which included Antonio's Wrangler. They climbed out of the Cherokee, all of them dressed for the occasion, more or less. Estelle wore a long, classy black dress, Manny an old blue suit, and Fernando a Harris Tweed blazer over his best pair of black slacks. Both Manny and Fernando wore bolo ties inset with black onyx stones.

Most of the attendees had gathered around the open grave further down the cemetery. Fernando spotted Luz, wearing her purple robes that in the sun made her look like royalty, queen of the Netherworld. Behind her stood Daniel, dressed in his usual jeans and polo shirt, and Francis Rose, dressed in a black business suit. Only Antonio hadn't dressed for the occasion, wearing jeans, a white shirt, and a leather vest. The big man stood talking to the two Rivera employees.

When Antonio saw them get out of the Cherokee, he smiled, waved, and came right over to greet them. "Long time no see," he said to Estelle and gave her a big bear hug.

"Nice to see you too, Antonio," Estelle said. "Sorry for the loss of your friend Jack."

Antonio thanked Estelle and then turned to Fernando, giving him a big bear hug too. He paused for a moment when he turned to Manny and then smiled, saying, "Oh, come on in here, you little punk," and swept Manny up in his arms like Manny was a little kid.

Manny laughed, embarrassed. He and Antonio weren't particularly fond of each other.

"Come on down, everything's ready," Antonio said, motioning down toward the open grave, where several folding chairs had been set up for the visitors in the aisles between rows of graves.

They followed Antonio into the cemetery and down the narrow dirt path to the open grave. As they came closer Fernando spotted the two musicians sitting in chairs on the opposite side of the grave from the mourners, Luz, Daniel, and Francis Rose. The two musicians turned out to be none other than the Haymakers, the husband and wife duo that he and Antonio had heard perform in the Sagebrush Inn Cantina several days earlier. As before the husband and wife looked identical, with stringy gray hair and sun-damaged faces. The only difference was that both were dressed in black. As before the wife held a fiddle, the husband a beat-up guitar, this one acoustic.

At the graveside everyone hugged everyone else, except Daniel, who kept his distance. Luz and Francis looked especially radiant in the bright sunshine, as did Estelle. Three elderly but gorgeous women, who put the sloppily dressed males to shame. After allowing sufficient time for greetings, the Rivera workers asked Antonio if they were ready to begin. Antonio nodded and motioned to the musicians. All of the guests gathered around the open grave.

On cue the Haymaker duo began playing and singing "Amazing Grace" and the guests all took their seats. Fernando and Estelle, the latest to arrive, sat at the very end of the row of chairs. "Finally," Fernando said. "We're finally done chasing Lacy and the ghost of Dennis Hopper."

"We'll all be ghosts soon enough...ghosts chasing ghosts," Estelle replied, sighing.

Fernando gave her a funny look.

Meanwhile the Rivera team slowly, solemnly carried Lacy's casket down the narrow trail to the grave. Using ropes, they lowered the casket into the ground and stood back.

Luz stood up and started the ceremony by tossing a handful of dirt on top of the casket. Then she faced the other guests and said: "We're here today not to mourn the loss of Jack Lacy, but to celebrate his transition. We honor his spirit, now free from the confines of his physical form. May it find peace and joy in the infinite realms. May his light continue to shine brightly in our hearts and in the world, a testament to the beauty of life's journey. We send him forth with love, peace, and the promise of eternal life. *Namaste*."

While the others congratulated Luz, Estelle elbowed Fernando and whispered, "That was beautiful. Who is she?"

"She's the curandera who helped Lacy cross over," Fernando replied. "Antonio hired her."

"Beautiful," Estelle said.

Now Antonio grabbed a handful of dirt and tossed it on the casket. He stood erect and began speaking softly, not his usual bark. "In spite of what you may have heard about Jack Lacy's profession, he was a good and decent man who made a living doing what he was trained to do. He was a top-rated sniper in the United States Marines who served in the first Iraq war. He was my friend and Marine buddy and saved my life on more occasions than I care to remember. After he left the Marines he went out of his way to help other wounded veterans. He donated large sums of money and did everything he could to help his fellow warriors, even when he knew he was dying of Glioblastoma from exposure to burning pit toxins in Iraq, which so many Iraq veterans contracted. Jack never felt sorry for himself, never complained about his death sentence. He was proud of what he'd done for his country."

Antonio looked at Fernando with pleading eyes. "Do you want to say a few words? Share your thoughts?"

Fernando had no interest in saying a few words, but Antonio had put him in a tough spot. So he stood up and cleared his throat, looking around at the gathered mourners. He grabbed a handful of dirt and tossed it on the casket, as Luz and Antonio had done. "Well, I will say one thing," he began. "Jack Lacy was hands-down the best shot I have ever seen. He single-handedly helped us defeat the Sinaloa Cartel when they showed up in Santa Fe a couple of years ago. For that all of us in Santa Fe and Northern New Mexico owe him a great debt."

"Very diplomatic," Estelle said with a wink when Fernando sat back down next to her.

Fernando laughed. "One of my very few talents—avoiding saying how I really feel."

No one else offered to speak, so Antonio stood up and motioned for the music to continue.

The guitarist—that is, the husband of the Haymaker duo—waved back. "Okay, here's a song that was dear to Jack Lacy and his friend Dennis Hopper. It's "The Ballad of Easy Rider," the theme song of the movie of the same name, written I think by the great Roger McGuinn of the Byrds. If you've seen the movie, then you'll surely remember the song—and the two motorcycles riding down the Taos highway through the beautiful national forest."

With that introduction, accompanied by his wife on fiddle, the two of them transitioned into the song:

"The river flows, it flows to the sea
Wherever that river goes
That's where I want to be
Flow, river, flow...."

While the music played, the guests talked among themselves. Fernando introduced Estelle to Luz and Francis Rose. The three women took an instant liking to each other, in what could have been a lesson for the three men. Antonio and Manny began chatting off to the side, a friendly exchange that surprised Fernando because the two of them had never really been friendly, mostly because Antonio was suspicious of the younger Manny.

Meanwhile, the Haymaker duo continued with "The Ballad of Easy Rider":

"All they wanted was to be free
And that's the way it turned out to be
Flow, river, flow...."

The music continued with one folk rock tune after another for a good fifteen or twenty minutes as the group of mourners began making their way out of the cemetery and into the parking lot, leaving the two Rivera workers to finish the burial. Luz and Daniel were the first to drive off, followed by Francis Rose. That left only Fernando, Estelle, and Manny to keep Antonio and the musicians company.

Finally the husband of the Haymarket Duo announced they would be ending their set with a fast, upbeat version of "The Ballad of Easy Rider," a fast, rock'n'roll version perfect for listening and dancing. Hearing this, Estelle did a couple of fancy dancing steps on her way to the parking lot. For a moment Fernando thought she was about to start dancing.

Antonio followed, bringing up the rear. The big man leaned back against his Wrangler, resting for a moment and trying to get his breath. He wiped his brow with his shirtsleeve and then said, "Thank God it's over, I'm exhausted. I hope Jack liked the ceremony today. Luz and I did our best. I don't know about the music. It was the best I could do on short notice. Somehow, though, it seemed appropriate. You know what I mean?"

"You did a great job, Antonio," Fernando said. "You're a good friend. The best. I'm really going to miss you."

Fernando gave Antonio a parting hug and then said, "If it's okay with you, I'm thinking about coming up to visit you this Spring or early Summer. Whenever it's convenient."

Antonio smiled. "That'd be great, you can meet my son. I don't know if I'll ever get back to Santa Fe, so you'll have to come up and see me. I'm selling my cabin in the Pecos. Guy from Albuquerque wants to buy it for a fishing cabin and is offering a good price, more than I ever expected to get for it. I'll miss Santa Fe and especially the Pecos, but my son needs my help, so what can I do?"

Fernando nodded. "Okay, I'll try to come up sometime in early May, before the highways fill up with tourists," Fernando said.

"That would be perfect—I'll put you to work on the ranch," Antonio said. "Lots to do that time of year."

Estelle laughed at that. "Hah! That's rich! I can't even get him to do yard work at home."

By this time Manny was already in the Cherokee, eager to leave, so Fernando and Estelle said their final goodbyes and joined Manny, just as the Haymaker duo returned to an up-tempo version of "The Ballad of Easy Rider:"
"Go, river, go
Past the shaded tree
Flow, river, flow
Flow to the sea,
Flow to the sea."

Fernando waved at Antonio and the musicians and then started the Cherokee. He eased out of the Jesus Nazareno parking lot onto Highway 518 and turned right toward Ranchos de Taos.

After turning on the highway he saw in his mind's eye the ghosts of Jack Lacy and Dennis Hopper, their elbows linked together, dancing spritely among the rows of graves to the music of the Haymakers.

For one brief moment everything was perfect in this fallen world.

READERS GUIDE

1. Who is Jack Lacy? Why has he come to Santa Fe? Why do so many people fear him?

2. Antonio Blake, who served in the Marines with Lacy, takes Lacy to Taos. Why?

3. Former Santa Fe Police Detective Fernando Lopez joins Lacy and Antonio in Taos. Why does he join them?

4. Lacy wants a curandera to conduct a crossover ceremony for him. Antonio finds a curandera named Luz to do the crossover ceremony. What is a crossover ceremony? What does a curandera do?

5. Lacy and Antonio stay at the Mabel Dodge Luhan House in Taos. What is the history of the Luhan House. Why do they stay there?

6. While staying at the Luhan House Lacy claims to see and converse with the ghost of Dennis Hopper. What is Lacy's connection to Dennis Hopper?

7. Does Fernando believe in ghosts? What about Antonio?

8. What all does Antonio do in Taos to satisfy Lacy's desire?

9. What happens at the crossover ceremony that disrupts their plans?

10. Who are Daniel and Art Stokes and what do they attempt to do? Does their scheme work?

11. What surprises Antonio and Fernando when they see Lacy's death certificate?

12. Why does Luz have to do a second crossover ceremony for Lacy.

13. Describe Lacy's funeral at Jesus Nazareno Cemetery. Is it successful?